You are the guest of honor at a Presidential conference. Protestors show up—with guns? Who do you trust, the beautiful brown-eyed boy, the mystical spirit-child, or the grizzly bear you talked to on a hike?

Fifteen-year-old Sammy Carlisle is hyper-excited. She will attend an environmental conference, meet the President, spend several totally magical days in Glacier National park, and say a few words about saving wildlife and the environment. When whisked away on a fifteen-mile hike, everything goes sideways.

On the trail, Sammy meets fascinating characters who trigger her empathic sensitivity and put her on alert. When protestors crash the conference, she is thrown into the center of a conspiracy filled with treachery and deceit.

As the conference crumbles into a mad rush for survival, the lines between good and evil, right and wrong, blur. "You are a puppet of the powerful," she is told, and for the first time, Sammy questions her loyalties and must make choices never imagined—the truth she once knew or the pull of her heart.

Now she must rely on her empathic sensitivity, her new friends, and a bear to save her.

Other Novels by Nickolai Vasilieff
Empath series:

Sea Whisperer
Alpha She Wolf

Soon to be released:
The Project

Loon Song Publishing, Portland, Oregon

Library of Congress Cataloging-Pending

Sammy and the San Juan Express, Presidential Bear: A novel / by

Nickolai Vasilieff — 1st ed.

Paperback: ISBN 978-0-9965070-4-2

—

Editor: Vera Haddan

For Seneca

without whose courage, beauty, kindness, tenacity,

and raw grit, I would not have found Sammy.

You are my inspiration.

JOIN THE SAMMY TEAM

Receive advance information on Sammy's Kindle, Audio, and paperback books, new stories, and special opportunities to read and review prerelease publications by signing up now at www.empathteen.com

If you enjoy Presidential Bear, please give us a review on Amazon.com and Goodreads.com. Visit www.empathteen.com , or search for *Empathteen, Presidential Bear, or Sammy and the San Juan Express.*

Presidential Bear

A Middle Grade / Young Adult Novel

Nickolai Vasilieff

Chapter One

S alt water spray brings tears to my eyes as I crest a twenty-foot swell. My sixteen-foot kayak holds. In the distance, I see the vanilla dome of Mt. Baker north of Seattle, but I'm nowhere near Seattle. The nose of my kayak crests, and drops off another peak, surfing the far side of the wave.

I left two hours earlier, angry at the world after being stuck in my room for weeks. The cold crisp air lets me know I am alive as I paddle out of Loon Song Harbor, on the southwest corner of Orcas Island. It's fantastic to be back on the water, but the weather changes fast in the San Juan Islands and in minutes, what was clear and cold becomes high winds and a blanket of fog so thick I can lick it.

I squint hard through occasional breaks. Only once do I spot Loon Song Harbor—a misty ghost in the distance. *You know better, Sammy,* I tell myself, *Uncle Teddy told you never to go out on the water alone,* especially after the last incident.

I hate talking about it, but my mother died earlier this year. On top of that, my brother, Loren, and I were shipped off to live with our Uncle Teddy on Orcas Island. And, on top of that, I was kidnapped (another story) when I tried to save sea lions and seals. For months after my mother's death, and weeks after the kidnapping and my own near death, I paced my room like a caged bear, ready to explode. I growled at anyone or anything that got in my way. This morning I woke at four, and by five I snuck out of the house and tiptoed to the docks. My gear was in our locker and my red kayak sat like a magic carpet, ready to take me away from my thoughts.

A wave breaks over the bow. I tip my right hip and lean into my paddle to hold the nose straight. My pulse pounds like a drum in my temples. The kayak skids into a trough between two massive rollers. Jaw clenched, I push my anger into the paddle as the enraged sea rolls over me. For a second I'm a sock tumbling in a giant washing machine. Sea foam smothers me. I rise up, gasping. My arms scream in pain as my paddle fights through the green-black ocean attacking me from all sides. The half dome compass spins past north. I reach another crest, and a wall of deep gray collapses around me. My mind freezes on the realization that I paddle blind.

Am I near rocks on my left that smash kayaks to smithereens, or am I in the narrows to my right with currents that sink even large ships in the San Juan Channel? What would Scooby do?

A gust of wind and a wave the size of Mt. Everest crashes over me. I breathe in a ton of salt water, cough and gag. Snotty water streams out my nose. Wind and surf turn my boat, and the next wave slams me sideways. The kayak tips to the left. I push the flat of the paddle onto the water to brace against rolling, but the kayak rolls anyway.

In the best of waters, paddling a kayak straight is exhausting, especially for a fifteen-year-old. Not that fifteen is young, but hey, give me a break, right now a straight course is impossible.

Lost and out of control, I prepare for the worst of all worsts—a total upside down dunking in some of the most dangerous water in the Northwest. One thought creeps through my mind:

I'm gonna die—either by drowning or Uncle Teddy's gonna kill me.

After my last excursion, four weeks ago, in a rental kayak, I pleaded with Uncle Teddy to buy me one. Okay, yes, I'd had some bad luck. A massive storm and strong currents carried me and my kayak out of Roche Harbor into the Spieden Channel. And yes, as strange as it sounds, rogue fisherman did kidnap me and try to kill me. But hey, look, I survived, and aside from the near-death experience, the kayaking was awesome.

After I recovered from the kidnapping and poisoning (yet another story), Uncle Teddy's response was, "No."

I don't mean kind of no, or even a maybe. I mean his face turned purple, his nostrils expanded like a caveman and his head almost spun off. He worried that after a near drowning in rough seas, a kayak of my own would mean more trouble.

"What can happen?" I asked. Wrong question. My ears burned from the list of a thousand things he yelled at me.

He must have said no a million times before he raised his hand above his head, slammed his San Juan Express cap on the dock, and yelled, "Okay, but only if you take classes, and never take the kayak out alone." I nodded in agreement as I danced with excitement. When he thought I was out of hearing, he added, "Teenagers!"

Now, I'm not in a class, but out on high seas with only a paddle, life vest, and my kayak. I roll far to the left and my instructor's words about capsizing ring in my ears.

"When you go over, lean forward and pull the loop at the front of your spray skirt. I call it the 'Oh Shit Loop.'" She said with a smile. "You'll find out why someday."

I lean forward and grip the loop as my shoulder dips into the icy water. One last deep breath, ready to go under for a butt-up dunking. Eyes scrunched tight, I think, *oh shit!*

Chapter Two

Air explodes in my lungs, but before I can pull the OS loop, I roll back and a waterfall gushes over my face. I wipe hair from my mouth and eyes. Instead of swimming with sharks, I'm sitting upright, and in the depth of my panic, a calm washes through me.

I know this place. It is a place of survival, like an infant must feel in the arms of its mother. I remember it from my last kayak adventure—the one Uncle Teddy warned me against—never go out alone. Only just like the last time, my friends are here to save me.

Beneath the dense fog, I spot a familiar white and black back along the left side of my kayak, and a four-foot-high dorsal fin cuts the surface. On my right a whiskered head pushes up with a snort. Oh my gosh, I've never been so happy to see my salt water friends, an Orca whale and a sea lion.

We rise and dip in twenty foot swells. The rollers keep coming. Salt spray and waves whip around me, but now, as I paddle, my two guardians guide me. Ocean fingers grab, push, and pull at my kayak, but my saviors shoulder the hull between their backs and keep me heading north. Exhausted, I lay back and relax into their sweet embrace.

My thoughts drift, and then Mom returns. She died a few months ago at our home in Portland Oregon. I helped take care of her and spent lots of time with her. I still can't believe my mother's gone, and in some ways, she's not. Since her death a million things have happened that I'm sure are from her. I don't know anything about afterlife or what happens when we die, but sometimes I hear her voice, and she reminds me that I'm special. Not important special, I don't mean that. I mean that I have, what she called, my special sensitivity. I feel animal's emotions. Not everyone believes me, but my friend Simone, a Marine Biologist, says I'm an empath. Sometimes I can even communicate with animals. They like me—what can I say?

Within minutes we reach the protection of Loon Song Harbor. My hair still whips my face, but the surface smooths to a windswept chop and the kayak knifes forward with ease. Ahead, Uncle Teddy's sea plane, Angie, rests on her moorage, perched like a giant cormorant, wings spread, at the end of the dock. Moving closer, the harbor comes into focus and so does the image of Uncle Teddy standing with binoculars focused on me. I wave. He does not wave back.

As if sensing the upcoming fireworks, my escorts lower beneath the surface and, more like stealth chickens than the ocean's greatest creatures, disappear.

Go ahead, run away. At least you could let him see you.

"I'm fine," I say, as I pull next to the boat mooring.

No response.

"I've been out for a half an hour or so. No big deal." I lay my paddle across the kayak and the dock to brace myself, then push up from my seated position and slide my butt onto the dock.

No response.

"When I left, the sky was clear, and then the fog rolled in. I came straight back. Really, I'm fine," I say forcing a smile.

Uncle Teddy stands frozen, arms crossed, eyes ice cube blue. "I thought we agreed you'd only go out with someone else?"

I struggle to twist my arm from my life jacket. "Yeah, but," *think quick Sammy.* I pull my kayak skirt over my head and feel the OS loop. "I had my friends with me. An Orca and a sea lion escorted me back."

Uncle Teddy looks into the water behind me, as if he expects to find a witness or something. He shakes his head, "I know with all that's happened you've been under a lot of stress, but this is not acceptable. I love you, Sammy, and I worry about you."

The ice cubes melt into a single tear that drips to his nose. He wipes his face, as if swiping at a fly. "Now isn't the time, with us leaving and all," he continues, "but we're going to have to figure out an arrangement to give you what you need, and keep me from having a heart attack."

I smile. "Yeah, I guess you're right. I'll be more careful. I promise."

He pauses. "I know you do. But promises don't mean much if you don't keep them."

His words sting like a slap in the face. I stare at my kayak, not wanting to look him in the eye. A spider of guilt crawls up my neck.

"We'll figure this out when we return," he says. "We have to leave in about an hour. Why don't you go change and grab your bags, while I get Angie ready."

In silence, I slide my kayak onto the dock. The plastic hull scrapes across the concrete deck, and I secure it with two straps. Uncle Teddy's the sweetest man I know. He loves me, and only wants the best for me, but I hate being judged. It's all I can do not to yell at him. Since my younger brother, Loren, and I were sent to live with him, I've been boiling. Like a volcano, I have this huge pit inside with magma building, ready to explode. Someone looks at me and I feel judged. When anyone asks how I am I just want to scream. One minute I can't sit still and the next I can't get my face off the pillow. And now, we're going to make a delivery to someone. I don't know where, and I'm not sure I even want to go.

Uncle Teddy reaches out to give me a hug. I start to pull back, but force myself to step forward. I rest my chin on his shoulder as he squeezes and pats my back. "It will get better," he says.

"What am I packing for?" I ask, without acknowledging his comment.

"Need to know," he says with a twinkle in his eye. "Just pack some warm clothes and make sure you have your boots. I'll fill you in as soon as we're in the air.

I swallow my flash of anger and turn on my heel. "I need to know everything," I say.

Chapter Three

Fishing boats bob in the harbor. Wind whips huge white sails coming and going, and the clanks of rigging on masts reach up the hill to my bedroom. Mixed in are stinkpots, Uncle Teddy's name for motorboats. Most of the boats are owned by locals, but every day a string of tourists pass through. They fuel up, buy supplies at the Loon Song Harbor Marina, and head out. From my bedroom, I see the tops of masts, taller stinkpots, and several islands across the San Juan Channel. Sometimes, like today, a wind so fierce it knocks you over will race across the strait, pulling up waves and thrashing boats and birds alike. On others, it's warm and calm and you can see for miles.

I slam my bedroom door and kick a pillow across the room. Why do I have to keep explaining myself? Just because no one else understands my empathic sensitivity doesn't mean animals don't help me. I jerk out two pairs of jeans from my dresser. They unfold, and one flops to the floor. A quick turn and I throw the other one at my roller bag. It slams into the headboard. I pull open a second drawer and grab a handful of underpants and socks. A quick flip and they fly around my bag like flower petals in a storm.

Simone, the Marine Biologist on San Juan Island who first introduced me to the resident Orca pods near the islands, understands me. She has empathic sensitivity too, although not as strong as mine. She says it's normal to sense animals or people's emotions. She says everyone does, but most humans are too wound up to notice it. "Slow down, honey child," she says, "and you'll sense all kinds of things."

Lately it's become kind of a problem with Uncle Teddy. He wants to protect me and because he can't hear the animals, he thinks I'm putting myself in danger, when I'm actually safe. I can't blame him. Who would think you're safe around wild animals? Most people would be in danger, but not me—most of the time.

My wavy reflection skims across the window. I push my hair out and it hangs straight, mud brown, over my shoulders. *Wish I had curly hair like Simone.* A few strands tickle my nose and I brush them back and wrap a band to make a pony tail. *If Mom were here, she'd do a reverse braid.* I slap the bed with my brush. *Why aren't you here?*

I stiffen and close my eyes, but it's no use. The tears begin. Half sadness, half rage—it just happens. I think of her or remember doing something with her and, like lava from deep inside my being, tears erupt. I hate it. I hate feeling alone.

With a t-shirt, I wipe my cheek. *Thoughts, that's all they are, just stupid thoughts.* The t-shirt wraps my nose and I blow. The snotty shirt lands on the floor. A few more blouses and my toiletries, and the bag is over full. I plant my butt on top and sit to close the zipper. The bag slides off the bed and hits the floor with a thud. *At least I get a few days away from Loon Song Harbor.* I take a deep breath. Jasmine incense mixed with pungent salt air swims around me. *All I need is a change and some activity.*

I grab my roller bag. Half way down the hall I remember my hiking boots. A minute later, boots slung over my shoulder, I kick the back door closed, slip through the dew-covered grass, and head for the dock.

Now I find out where the heck I'm going.

Chapter Four

My hand twists as the roller bag catches a rock, skips sideways, and tips over, "crap." The metal gangplank leading to the dock creaks as I lift the bag, and drop it on its wheels. Seriously, the bag weighs a ton.

"Hurry up," a squeaky voice says from behind.

I tense and straighten. It's everything I can do not to yell at him, or pinch him, or anything to get rid of him. But, with all that has happened, I know the Dorkster hurts too. And, after all, he's the only brother I have. Loren pushes his shoulder into my waist and moves past. I look down on his multi-colored baseball cap. A purple, plastic propeller spins on top. One of the few things that make me smile is seeing what clown-boy is wearing. Since we moved to Loon Song Harbor, Loren dresses in the most ridiculous combinations of patterns and colors. It's not like he doesn't have matching clothes, but he creates clown suits out of everything—blue pants, bright orange t-shirt with a picture of Sasquatch on the back, yellow tennis shoes, and his whirligig hat. *Maybe he's color blind.* The ramp bounces as he skips down and hops on the dock, knees bent, arms out in his totally corny super-hero pose.

"Good morning," a second voice reaches me with a laugh. "He's full of spunk this morning."

"Good morning," I say to Liz. "Spunk's one word for it." I hesitate. "Was he at your place last night?"

"No," her cheeks flush pink. "I woke him when I heard you packing."

"You were at the house?"

"Yes." She watches me, searching for a hint of judgment or approval, then smiles and looks down.

Even standing below her on the ramp, I am taller. I've grown so much in the past year and next to her I feel skinny and weird. Her blond hair halos her face. I smile back. "I don't care," I say. "I know you and Uncle Teddy are together."

She coughs and shuffles her feet like she's sweeping the deck. "Thanks. We haven't talked and I wasn't sure. This is the first time I've stayed over since you arrived."

I step forward and reach out. The handle slips. The roller bag slaps hard against the ramp again and thumps a few feet away. We both jump. "It's okay. I don't mind," I say, but I do mind. Her happiness is like a stick poking at my loneliness, and I want some of what she has.

Liz and her father, Olie, own the Loon Song Harbor dock and store only a block from Uncle Teddy's … our house. I figured out Liz and Uncle Teddy were dating shortly after I arrived, but they'd kept their relationship on the down-low until last night. I guess with Uncle Teddy and me leaving, and her staying at the house to watch Loren, she decided to come out of the closet with their, not-so-secret, secret.

"I've been meaning to ask you," Liz says, "I know these past several months have been difficult, do you still want to work at the store?"

When I first came to the islands, Liz asked me to work at her store. Maybe she sensed my isolation in a house with two boys, or felt my loss. Either way, it kept me busy. With my rehab from the injuries during the kidnapping, I haven't worked for several weeks.

"Yes," I blurt, "of course. Is there something wrong? Did I do something?"

"No, no, it's nothing like that. I just wanted to be sure, and to let you know that I want you to work with me."

Her words wash through me, warm and comforting. The truth is, she fills the emptiness in my gut, and I've begun to think of her like an older sister. I pick my bag up and start down the ramp, "Are you kidding?" I say, "I totally like this capitalism thing. Work—money—buy stuff. I like how that works."

"Yes, I know." she says with a chuckle. "You're an excellent consumer."

"Got your gear packed?" Uncle Teddy says as I pass toward Angie. "You sure you're up for this? Your new BFF is dying to see you, but we can always make it another time."

"BFF?" I say, intrigued that I might learn something about our trip.

"The President."

With raised eyebrows, I say, "So that's who were going to see. The President isn't my BFF", I add, "and yes, I'm fine. How many times are you going to ask me that?"

His head turns and the muscles in his jaw lock.

"I'm sorry," I say. "I'm fine. Where are we going, anyway?"

My question distracts him. "Nice try," he says. "Need to know, remember."

Need to know—need to know. You'd think we were on a top-secret mission or something. The President heard about my trying to save seals and sea lions, and the capture of fishermen who were killing them to protect their salmon catch. He sent me some flowers and called to congratulate me. He said we'd get to meet, but I didn't think it would be this soon.

"Yhaaa," the Dorkster yells as he jumps around Angie, posed like a Jedi knight. He swings an imaginary sword above his head and dances in front of me. Uncle Teddy laughs and the tension relaxes. In my best Princess Leia, I take three steps forward and bend in the traditional sword fighting pose, "Hyaa," I yell. He rushes me, shoes scraping across the dock, until he trips and stumbles. Inches from a face plant, I reach forward and catch him. His arms wrap around my waist and his face pushes into my belly.

"Are you leaving?" he mumbles through the hug.

OMG, the little dork still irritates me to death, seven-year-old brothers are the worst, but things have changed. Without Mom and Dad, I'm all he has. When I hug him, at times, he actually hugs me back. Today's truce lasts only a moment, until he pushes back, "Where are you going?"

"Not sure," I say, putting him in a headlock. "Uncle Teddy says, need to know, and won't tell me."

Loren snorts, "Need to … hyaa." He jerks loose and cuts me in half with his imaginary sword. "I want to go."

"Can't." I duck, his pretend sword attacking my head.

Then he gets serious, a whiny kind of serious. "Why not? I want to go too. I never get to go anywhere."

I lower my head, trying to look sympathetic. "I know. It's not fair, but I can't take you on this trip. It's just for … me. Besides, it's only three days and probably won't be any fun—nothing exciting happening."

"You're going to see the President. I know what you're doing."

"We might see the President? You know more than I do. But if he's there, it will be for other reasons, not me."

The imaginary sword drops and his head lops to one side in pitiful defeat.

"Tell you what, when I get back, we'll go on an adventure, hunt real pirates or something. I promise."

It's hard, but the Dorkster holds his pose, even when I say pirates. I laugh. He looks up. "It's not funny," but he cracks a smile.

"Gotcha," I say as Uncle Teddy approaches.

"Are we all ready?" He ruffles Loren's hair.

"Ready as I'll ever be," I say.

I notice Liz sneak up behind Loren and grab his ribs. He jumps and giggles as she puts him in a bear hug and swings around. The truth is that I feel guilty and a little jealous. While she became my sister, Liz became Loren's surrogate Mom, and, although I'd never dream of acting like Mom, I kind of like his fleeting attention, I guess. Even so, knowing she watches over him makes leaving a lot easier. I turn to step into Angie.

"Wait, wait," Loren screams.

He wriggles from Liz's grasp. Bends forward, and struggles to pull something from his pant pocket.

"I have something for you," he mutters, as his fist pops up. "Close your eyes."

I study his mischievous little face, and with skepticism, shut my eyes.

"Don't peek," he orders.

My open hand slides forward, anticipating a worm or worse. The dock rocks, and water sloshes beneath us. A seagull squawks and I feel a cool, solid round object rest in my palm. *Poop* is my first thought, but it's too solid.

"Okay, open your eyes. It's my compass from my spy kit," he says, bouncing up and down. "You might need it to find your way home."

I hiccup and swallow to hold back a tear.

"You have to give the compass back though. I need it for my kit."

I reach out to hug him, but he jumps back in a sword fighting pose.

"I'll bring it back, Punkster," I say. "I'll keep it right here in my pocket." I slide the smooth directional device into my pocket and pat it, treating it like the sacred instrument he thinks it is.

In Angie, I feel the cavern of emptiness return. My eyes reach out to Loren; I want to hug him one more time. He isn't paying attention, of course. He wrestles with Liz. *It's okay,* I tell myself. *You'll be back in three days. What can happen in three days?*

Chapter Five

Like an old woman clearing her throat, Angie's engine coughs twice. Her huge propeller catches and spins. Liz and Loren step back to the ramp, hands raised to shield their eyes. My body vibrates to the roar, as blade tips create circles of speed in front of me. Uncle Teddy pushes the throttle, and the noise increases. My stomach turns tiny cartwheels as Angie rolls down the short incline and bobs on the water. Propeller spray spreads around us. Ducks and geese flee our attack and seagulls retreat above. I search the water. *Are my friends, the Orca and sea lion, anywhere near?*

We increase speed and my head and shoulders push back. We leave the harbor and Angie lifts, her long pontoons slapping the waves. I glance out the side window; finger-like whitecaps hold her until the last moment. My chin bounces against my chest two, three times, and, like a bullet leaving a barrel, Angie shoots off the surface. We rise above the sparkling blue of Loon Song Harbor and the green of the San Juan Islands.

Angie's right wing lowers. We circle, and zoom back over the dock. Uncle Teddy waggles her wings to say good-bye, and I wave at two tiny bodies. The Dorkster, in his clown outfit, jumps up and down, swinging his hat. Liz gazes up, sun reflecting off her sunglasses. Angie's cool glass side window presses against my forehead as our shadow passes over them. Loren shrinks behind me. His image jiggles to the rhythm of the vibrations, and the pit grows in my belly, like I might never see him again. Before the last couple of months, such a thought never crossed my mind. Now it haunts me. "I love you," I whisper to the window, and he is gone.

On a map, Orcas Island looks like a horseshoe with the legs pointed down. Loon Song Harbor sits in the lower left corner. Within minutes we pass the island and soar over the mainland. Mount Baker rises almost eleven thousand feet to our left. To our right, giant Mount Rainier peaks at almost fifteen thousand feet, still wearing a pure white cap. Farther south, a string of mountains called the Cascade Range line up like school children with pointy white witch's hats.

I hear, "665 alpha romeo, heading eight seven, at niner five thousand, leaving …," before my headset slips off, and the gibberish in my ears is replaced by the roar of air rushing past sheet metal, a thousand vibrations and the growl of Angie's massive engine.

Uncle Teddy points, "We're headed six hundred miles east to the Rocky Mountains."

"Great," I say and wipe my nose on my jacket. "Now will you tell me where we're going?"

His laughter fills the cockpit, "I guess this is as good a time as any ... Glacier National Park, along the Canadian border in northern Montana."

I push loose strands of hair behind my ear and adjust my sun glasses, "A park on a glacier?"

"No, more like a park with lots of glaciers in it."

I wait, and when he doesn't say anymore I ask, "So we'll land on a glacier?"

He nudges the throttle and Angie's nose lifts. We sail over a valley between mountains on either side. "No, we're headed to a resort hotel, in the far corner of the park, called Many Glacier Lodge. The lodge sits next to Swiftcurrent Lake. We'll put her down at the far end of the lake and deliver our load."

I jerk to attention, "Load?"

The last time he told me we were delivering "a load," we picked up a sea lion and transported her, in Angie, to the San Juan Islands. We almost died when she broke from her cage. Loren, Uncle Teddy, and I fell into the freezing water of the Strait of Juan de Fuca. The sea lion, later, saved my life and became my friend. Although I've encountered other sea lions, I've only seen her a few times since then.

Uncle Teddy peeks at me from the corner of his eye, playing with me. I used to love his teasing, but now, I become angry, like he means to make fun of me or something.

"Well?" I persist, "Are we picking up another sea lion?"

With his right hand, he adjusts a small wheel on the dashboard and Angie's tail lifts. He inspects a few of the instruments, and pretends to fix his hair. After an eternity, with a sly smile, he says, "Well, actually, we're delivering ... seafood, and you, of course."

"Seafood? Like oysters and salmon or something?"

"Yup. Like oysters and salmon and stuff."

Again, he squints at the dashboard, but before his fingers reach his hair I take a swing at his arm. "Com'on, what are we doing for my new BFF?"

"Hah," he explodes, "he is your BFF."

Sometimes Uncle Teddy can be totally irritating like fingernails on a chalk board. "I just said BFF because you said BFF. Tell me, what does the President want us to do?" I turn away from him.

Below, the tree covered Cascade Range transitions into yellow grassland. The thin needle on Angie's altimeter points at ten thousand, five hundred feet.

"Don't let this go to your head," he says. "You're requested to attend a conference the President is giving for a few friends."

I turn back to face him. Even when he irritates me, I don't stay mad for long. He always wears his Navy leather flight jacket when he flies, and with his blond hair splayed out from under his San Juan Express cap, he looks awesomely cool.

"A conference? Friends?" I ask.

"They're called the G-20, and they're meeting on the environment and Climate Change. He wants to introduce you as the hope of the next generation or something."

The last time I flew in Angie I peed my pants. For good reason, we almost hit a bridge, and it almost happened again. Peed my pants, that is. "You're kidding; introduce me to a bunch of ...? What is the G-20 anyway?"

"Don't worry. They are only leaders from the twenty most powerful nations in the world."

"OMG! Introduce me to twenty world leaders. I brought jeans and boots."

"Don't worry. They emailed a dress code and Liz did some shopping last week. I have a bag in the back with dresses, blouses, skirts, shoes and a million other things, so you can choose your wardrobe—Your Highness."

Your Highness sounds good. "So we're going to a conference?"

"Yes, for two days, but we're a day early, so we can do some exploring. He will introduce you on the morning of the second day."

Here, ladies and gentleman, I imagine he will say, *is the next Queen of the World.*

Chapter Six

Adeer's head rises, startled by the crack of a branch under heavy boots. She stops chewing, and in a moment, bolts through Aspen and dense brush.

"Ark," a small man calls from behind, "let us have break. We push hard for three hours and my feet, they kill."

The taller man swings his six foot six frame toward the voice. His squinted gaze targets the smaller man whose pack already slides to the ground. The urge to punch Nakale rushes through Ark's veins like boiling water. He steps forward.

"He's right," says a third man, interrupting Ark's impending attack. "We are not all like you, able to cover ten miles in two hours, and all of it off trail. If we were, we would march forever. But we are mortals, now is a good time for a rest."

Ark's black eyes stare from deep set sockets and shift from Nakale to Samuel—his second in command. Samuel's curly chestnut brown hair, brilliant smile, and easy manner humor Ark. With a swing of his shoulder, Ark lowers his backpack to the ground. "Ten minutes, and we march," he orders. "Do not forget, we are not here for a vacation. We have a job to do."

North of Glacier National Park, in Southern Canada, morning shadows surround the small clearing. Eighty pound packs drop onto pine needles from the four hikers, three men and one woman. The slim woman, dressed in army fatigues, long black hair wrapped in a tight brown turban, glances at Nakale and giggles in a mocking manner. An AR-15 automatic rifle rests in the crook of her right arm.

"Shut up Fatuma," Nakale protests. As he barks at Fatuma, he shifts his weight and loose gravel moves under his boot. Nakale stumbles, trips on his backpack and somersaults onto his back.

Fatuma's giggles explode into full scale laughter, "Oh Nakale, you are the best comedian I've ever seen. Are you sure you weren't in the circus before you became a so-called assassin?"

Nakale grunts and rolls. Seeing Nakale's anger, Fatuma steps closer to Ark, but not too close, and moves her right hand to the pistol grip of her rifle. Eyes darting from Ark to Fatuma, Nakale's fingers scratch the dirt like an angry bull. Head down, he sprints toward Fatuma. High up in an Aspen tree, a Great Horned owl swivels her head backward to watch the commotion.

Once again Samuel, the peace maker, steps in to unravel the tension. "All right, she means nothing," he says, "just a bit of fun." He gives a gentle, but firm, push on Nakale's shoulder, throwing Nakale off course. He slips and again goes down on the gravel. Fatuma's laughter echoes through the forest as she releases her fingers from the grip. The owl spreads its spotted wings, leaves its perch, and swoops toward a friendlier enclave.

From the edge of the clearing, Ark studies his three soldiers with questioning eyes. *Did I make the right choices? Are they ready? Will the mission succeed?* Each one was handpicked for this mission. He trained them for almost four months, but it was barely time to familiarize them with their objective, let alone reeducate them in the philosophy of Mao's true socialist manifesto.

My hope was to make them my small army, he recalls. *Instead, they are nothing more than a disorganized and undisciplined mob of children—children who can kill, to be sure.*

The others who went before, the ones who managed to obtain jobs as waiters and as a cook at the much too grand capitalist playground called Many Glacier Lodge, they too are trained well enough. Ark smiles at the remembrance of those original recruits, seven young fanatics who joined him almost a year ago. He instructed them in the fine art of deception, taught them how to apply for positions at the hotel, and furnished them with forged citizenship papers and job histories. Eventually, five of the seven were hired by the hotel and, although only three passed security screenings, they are enough. Those three heroes now work in the hotel, and are willing to die for the cause.

Only I could have done this, he muses as he flicks a large black fly off his knee. *And, if we are on time, they will create the diversion we need, and we will take control of the building.*

As Ark wallows in his own compliments, a skittering in the forest floor calls his attention to Nakale, who sits on a fallen log. There is movement behind the log. Two furry paws reach up and, three feet from Nakale, a black bear cub pops its head up. Ark is fascinated with the furry intruder, and as he considers whether or not to warn Nakale, a second set of paws reach up. A bear cub, no bigger than a poodle, pulls up on the log. Ark snorts a laugh. Samuel, also enchanted by the baby guests, steps forward. Nakale, eyes closed, swats at the sound next to him and hits the cub, knocking it off the log. Nakale turns and freezes.

"Found your bear," Ark says, laughing.

"Scared of a little teddy bear?" Fatuma says from a safe distance.

"Shut up," Nakale says. He carefully lifts his pack. Stay calm and make slow movements, he remembers reading. Ten feet from the log, a third head, the size of a large pumpkin, rises. She chews on long huckleberry branches and spots Nakale. Her mouth, the size of an oven door, opens and a freight train roar emerges. Forgetting the, stay calm, instructions, Nakale turns. "Bear, bear," he repeats as he sprints to a position behind Ark, who stands with gun in hand.

Mama bear swings her massive head back and forth. Satisfied with the group's reaction, she yanks another stalk from the huckleberry bush, and saunters into the woods.

The two cubs chase after her, rolling over each other, and darting to avoid her massive paws.

The four Scorpions sigh in collective relief as the bears leave the clearing. Nakale remains hunched behind Ark. Fatuma stands near a tree she used for protection. Samuel remains in the clearing, only yards from where the mother bear had been. Ark scratches a mole on his nose. His almost total confidence in Samuel is reconfirmed by Samuel's lack of fear around the bear. That he is Ark's most trusted soldier is obvious to everyone. They met a year earlier, in Montreal Canada. Ark would later explain to other recruits, "I stood on a street corner, lecturing to anyone who would listen about the demonic forces of Capitalism, when a handsome young man appeared, handing out pamphlets for the local Communist Party. I recognized Samuel's strength and determination at once, and approached him. 'You waste your time giving out flyers when you could be changing the world,' I told him. He listened and after a few meetings over coffee, Samuel made the right choice. He realized his destiny lie with Arkimedes Litvinov and the Black Scorpions."

A tiny, illuminated, analog watch clicks second by second on Ark's wrist. The flash of a passing second interrupts his thoughts. "It's time," he yells, and with one jerk hoists his backpack to his shoulder and stands. A ground squirrel leaps to safety as Samuel finishes a swig of water and lifts his pack in place. Fatuma slides her arm through a strap and swings her heavy pack up. Nakale, the only one to hesitate, grunts his disapproval. With a knee to his shoulder, Samuel lifts Nakale's backpack and forces him to stand. "It's time," Samuel says.

Loose pebbles surrender under Ark's fast steps as the sun crests the horizon and the air warms. With lengthy strides, Ark races forward. Sweat drips from Fatuma's chin as she runs, determined to reach the ridge first. Ark glances back and quickens his pace. He enjoys her humor and respects her ruthless determination. Captured as a child by the Revolutionary United Front in Sierra Leone, Fatuma was taken to Liberia and put into slavery. Years later, while serving as a mercenary soldier for government forces, Ark freed her. When reminded, he shakes his head and feigns humility.

"I did nothing. With three men, we simply attacked the house filled with twelve guards. They ran, and we liberated the sixteen women inside."

A year later, when Ark applied for immigration to Canada, he brought Fatuma as his wife. He knows she loves him, but his feelings could never be described as love—he loves no one, other than himself. "But," he often reminds himself, "she is an expert markswoman and a ruthless killer. As a bonus, she would die for me."

Farther back, Nakale adjusts his pack, which measures half his size, and slips to one knee on the gravel. Watching the boy struggle under his load reminds Ark of how he found Nakale on the streets of Montreal, Quebec. He does not know for sure, but Ark guesses Nakale was no more than fourteen years old at the time. It took months for Ark to gain Nakale's trust. He later learned that Nakale had been a child soldier, trained and forced to protect illegal diamond mines in Angola. He was rescued by United Nations forces and brought to Canada as a refugee. Although he has no formal education, Nakale is an expert in street smarts. Ark has seen him break down and reassemble a rifle in minutes, and shoot the eye out of a rat at one hundred yards. He is quick like a cat, and, for the most part, follows orders. His biggest problems—he is lazy, angry, and, to Fatuma's amusement, he is clumsy. At times, Nakale's youth triggers a curious pang in Ark's chest—the closest he comes to sympathy. But normally, Ark feels nothing but mild curiosity that Nakale, a child, fights so hard to be treated like a man.

A single burp of laughter bubbles up Ark's throat when Nakale collapses under his pack, yet he is disturbed. On this mission, the most important of his life, one mistake might mean failure. Ark shakes his head and quickens his stride as Fatuma approaches. Uncertainty disturbs and angers him. Now is not the time to question my earlier decisions, he thinks. We are only a few miles from the border, well beyond the point of no return. This operation is a go, at any cost.

Ark moves fast enough to reach the summit seconds before Fatuma. *I am not a loser*, he reminds himself. Without looking back, but with a slight smile of satisfaction, he begins the descent toward the invisible United States border. Minutes later, Nakale scrambles on hands and knees to the crest with Samuel right behind.

Heat and the smell of pine rise up from the forest bed. A small arachnid raises its pointed tail and scurries beneath a rotted mushroom. Without passports or visas, and nameless as ghosts, the Black Scorpions creep their way through back country forests, into Glacier National Park.

"Remember," Ark spits over his shoulder, "we are dedicated to one mission, to cut off the head of the dragon."

Chapter Seven

I'm jarred awake by an intense vibration, like riding over a rough road. My stomach rises as we clear the nearest peaks of Montana's Rocky Mountains and Uncle Teddy pushes the yoke forward. Angie, like a trained dolphin completing the last half of a jump, dips her nose and begins a sharp descent leaving my stomach at ten thousand feet.

I choke back a sharp shriek and push my cheek against the cold side window. What I see steals my fear. Below are several lakes, the deepest turquoise in the center graduating to white at the edges. I must have said something because Uncle Teddy says, "Turquoise. They're filled with glacier water. Something about the particles in the water makes them appear more brilliant than normal lakes."

We drop altitude like a skydiver without a parachute and pass over a small glacial lake on a high plateau. A stream snakes to a cliff and tumbles like a thousand feet down. We zoom past the falls, and follow, at the bottom, a river that cuts through a red rock canyon. Our altitude decreases for several minutes, and, as we pass over another cliff, Uncle Teddy dips one wing and throws Angie into a steep right turn.

"Chinook One, landing 270, three miles out," he says. "Repeat, Chinook One, landing 270, three miles out, over."

My brow scrunches in a question mark. The plane's name is Angie and his call sign is N665AR. "Who's Chinook One?" I ask.

He laughs, "Special code. The Secret Service gave it to me when they authorized our coming to this conference." He twists the wheel and Angie makes a swift turn to the left. Dead ahead sits a row of tall trees, and beyond, another lake. Even I can tell; if we're high enough to clear the tree tops, we'll be way too high to make a water landing on the lake. My hand is white knuckled on the handhold above my head. I flinch, "Don't get too close," I say, pressing one knee against the dash panel.

"I'll do my best," he says and pushes the steering yoke. Angie's nose drops. Air from her wings rustles the tree tops, and we go into a seriously steep roller coaster dive. One moment I see tips of trees, the next, aquamarine of lake water approaching me at a million miles an hour. I scream and think, *we're gonna to die.* Before my body catches up with my brain, we level off and fly only feet above the mild chop of a long narrow lake. I relax my death grip on the hand hold until I see a brown multistory building at the end of the lake growing larger and larger. Uncle Teddy cuts the throttle and the free-spin whir of Angie's propeller replaces the engine noise. He pulls her nose up and Angie stalls.

Uncle Teddy explained a stall to me on my first fight with him, when I also screamed several times and, yes, peed my pants (just once). "When the angle of attack is increased to the point that lift is decreased," he said, "the plane drops from the sky."

I cover my face with my hands and have the ever-reoccurring thought: *OS, I'm gonna* … In that moment, Angie slaps the surface, hop scotches fifty feet and slaps down again. The seatbelt cuts into my shoulder. I brace against the dash and Angie comes to a stop. *I'm alive.* We bob like fish bait. Uncle Teddy removes his headset and with his totally irritating smile says, "We have a welcoming committee."

I peel my hands off my face and see Many Glacier Lodge flash beyond Angie's propeller spin. Two speed boats race toward us. A man squats behind a huge gun mounted on the bow of each boat. Another man stands farther back, holding a rifle.

"What's happening?" I say, my eyes the size of pie plates.

"Secret Service," he says, "I hope."

Waves slap against Angie's pontoons. The boats circle us once, then twice, and come to a stop on either side. Before we can unlatch the doors a soldier from each boat jumps on a pontoon and jerks the pilot and passenger doors open.

A man in a flak jacket, helmet, and carrying several guns, holds his hand out to Uncle Teddy, "Identification."

My stomach gurgles. A gush of freezing cold air rushes in and the smell of stale cigarettes reaches out from the uniform next to me.

With two fingers Uncle Teddy reaches inside his flight jacket and produces a letter and his license.

The soldier inspects the ID, hands it back to Uncle Teddy, and directs his gaze to me. "Please tell me your name, ma'am."

My mouth is dry. I cough and take a deep breath. I've never been called ma'am before. "Samantha Harriet Carlisle," I say. My voice shakes.

He scans his list and holds his hand out. "ID please."

My hand moves toward my pocket, and I realize I have no ID. I shrug and glance at Uncle Teddy.

"I'm afraid she doesn't have any identification," he says. "She just moved and ..."

"Wait a minute," I interrupt. "Uncle Teddy gave me a smart phone about a month ago and as a surprise he had my name engraved on it."

I pull out the phone and hand it to the agent. He reads the inscription and his stone face cracks into a partial smile. "I'm sure this will do, Miss Carlisle."

"I'm Lieutenant Blunk," he says, his face softer and his voice less gruff. "I'll escort you to the shore and secure your airplane." It turns out he had been in the Navy about the same time as Uncle Teddy, and they yak all the way about the, "good ol' days." At the edge of the lake, Uncle Teddy guns the engine and Angie skids up on a grassy bank. The engine pops and chugs to a stop as Lieutenant Blunk hops off the pontoon and motions to other agents standing nearby. Thankfully the stinky soldier leaves as well.

A group of three Secret Service men and two women crawl all over Angie as soon as we step out. A German Shepherd pokes his nose in the air then jumps inside Angie, sniffing for drugs or bombs. Who knows? As the K-9 unit pulls back, agents unload our boxes packed with dry ice and seafood. I lean to lift my bag and realize I might need permission. A man, with broad shoulders and the squarest jaw I've ever seen, nods his approval and I yank my backpack over my shoulder and pull the handle out on my roller bag. Behind me I hear—wobble, wobble, wobble.

"Hold on, Sammy." Uncle Teddy wheels over a cart that looks more like a coach than a luggage carrier. It's not a wheelbarrow, like we have at Loon Song Harbor. It's elegant, with a flat carpeted surface and brass corner posts. Each post rises up about five feet and curves in at the top. There's a small crown in the middle.

"Fancy dancy," I say.

"For my lady," he responds as he extends his arm and makes a big bow. I stand for a moment and he adds, "You still have to load your own bags."

"Is that any way to treat royalty?" I say, and throw my back pack and bag on the cart.

"Wait till you see your room," he chuckles.

Chapter Eight

A few feet behind, the click of a Secret Service agent's heels stalk us while Uncle Teddy pushes the luggage cart up a narrow path. Mid-morning sun throws shadows of the lodge on the lake, and I shiver from the chill. To our left stands a cliff where I imagine grizzly bears forage for huckleberries. A breeze whispers through the mountain tops, and small waves flash silver and gold across the water's surface behind us.

The entry, two heavy wood doors, opens into one end of a kitchen. On my left, my hand sweeps across a long cool stainless steel counter surrounded by mixers, cabinets, stoves and two wall height refrigerators. The ripping sound of box cutters comes from the corner as people in white chef uniforms cut open the boxes we brought and fill the refrigerator. To one side, a woman with a broad smile and a wilting chief's hat lifts spoons full of batter onto baking sheets, and the room is filled with a warm toasty smell from something baking in the oven. It's been hours since I had breakfast. I picture huckleberry muffins caked with cream cheese, and I look for something I might sneak off the table—nothing. On the right, a passage leads into a storeroom, and an elevator ahead. As we move through the kitchen, my toe catches and I stumble into the wall. A sharp pain shoots through my shoulder and trickles of blood drip down my arm. Unlike the outside structure, the walls on this level are rough concrete, painted light yellow, and textured like wood planks. I sweep my index finger across the scratches on my arm and lick. I've no idea why I do that; maybe it's the vampire in me. The blood is warm and has a metallic taste.

"You okay?" Uncle Teddy asks, as the luggage carrier wobbles into the elevator. My finger still in my mouth, I nod and follow him past an agent holding the door.

In jerking movements, we climb two levels. The door rattles open exposing a mud tan hallway. The dark floor and trim squeeze me with a claustrophobic sense of being an oversized Alice in Wonderland, and the smell changes from muffins to a sock drawer that hasn't been opened for ages.

"This hotel must be really old," I think out loud.

"About 1915," the Secret Service agent says, as he hands us ID tags on strings to hang around our necks. Down the hall, Uncle Teddy wheels the cart to the side and hands me a key attached to a rectangular piece of wood. Twenty-seven—it reads on one side—on the other it has a burned image of the hotel with the words, "Many Glacier Lodge."

The pitted and scratched key's weight surprises me. I juggle it with the ID Tag and almost drop it.

"Go ahead," Uncle Teddy points to the door and giggles. I hesitate and raise an eyebrow. "No, no, no-jokes. It's just your room."

I slip the key in the lock and turn. Without my touching the door knob, the latch clicks, and the door swings open. I gasp.

"What do you think?" he asks.

Suddenly, I'm a normal size Alice entering a queen's chamber. Light, through high windows, sweeps onto custard cream walls. A long pale green dresser stretches under sheer chiffon curtains, and a matching cabinet stands in the corner. The bed, the size of a swimming pool, pushes against the far wall, with a white comforter embroidered with red and gold leaves. Corner posts rise up, supporting a cloth canopy in the same pattern. Thankfully, the room smells of fresh pine and lavender.

"Well? Well?" he says, sounding more like Loren waiting to open a birthday present, than my uncle.

"I'm speechless."

"The President ordered it especially for you … My Lady."

I'm sure I have a smile as big as the moon when I spin around and fall backward on the bed. "Ouch." My head hits a mattress as hard as Papa Bear's bed. I wish for my soft down mattress at home.

The cart barely fits through the doorway as Uncle Teddy wheels our luggage into my room. "What's in this thing?" he asks when he unloads my bag, "rocks?" He opens the closet door, and when I think he is going to put my bag in, he instead pushes the cart into it.

"Got the wrong door, don't ya?" I ask.

"It's a door into my room. Isn't this great?" His voice disappears into his bedroom, "We've got adjoining rooms."

OMG. My head falls back on the hard mattress.

"Great," I say, with as much enthusiasm as I can muster. "Absolutely great."

My room looks out at the sheer cliff on one side and the lake on the other. The lake is beautiful but the cliffs rising to the North feel dark, almost sinister. My skin crawls as I study the flat gunmetal gray stone face that extends hundreds of feet above me. I stamp my feet to shake off the creepy crawlies as Uncle Teddy cranes his head around the door.

"Adjoining rooms doesn't mean we won't have our privacy." He reaches for a twist knob above the door handle and turns to demonstrate the dead bolt. "We have locks on both sides. I'll keep mine unlocked, but you can do as you like with yours. And, let's agree to knock before we enter each other's room, like at home."

"Agreed," I say, "and thanks. I appreciate the privacy."

He smiles and holds out a long flat box with a red bow. "I have something for you."

I imagine roses, or possibly a wand with a tiny crown at the end. "Thanks, but you've already given me more than you should," I say in my most humble voice.

His mouth falls half open, exposing his front teeth. He mumbles a few incoherent words, then says, "No, no, this is for your BFF when you see him."

I make a face like, you have to be kidding.

"Go on. It's a necktie Liz bought. She thought you might like to give him something."

I take the box, "A necktie? Isn't that kind of lame?"

"Not really. It has a great picture of a salmon on it. It'll be a keepsake from the Pacific Northwest."

It gets awkward as I stand frozen and stare at his totally weird gift and he adds, "Let's get changed. There's still time for a long hike."

"Hike?" I drop the box on the bed. "I was just getting comfortable, sort of."

He turns, hiking poles fly out of his other hand and clank on the floor. "C'mon, put those new boots to use." He holds up two bags. "And, I had lunch delivered."

The word, "lunch," triggers a brain-body response. My knees weaken and my clothes suddenly feel like they are made of chain-mail. My energy drops through the floor.

"Okay." I say. "Lunch first, then hike."

Uncle Teddy tosses a brown bag on the bed and, like a ravenous wolf, I tear the bag open, shred the sandwich wrapper, and scarf down the turkey sandwich in four bites. The cookie is consumed in one chomp. Uncle Teddy sits horrified on my bed, and holds his unwrapped sandwich behind his back. Protecting it from me, I assume.

Licking my lips, I spot the torn bag on the floor with the clear wrap in pieces. I shrug, "What can I say? I was hungry."

"Put your hands in the air and step away from my lunch bag," he says, back peddling toward his bedroom and keeping his body between me and that second delicious sandwich.

"Cookie. I love cookie," I say as he disappears behind his door and I hear the dead bolt latch.

My shoelaces are like two feet too long. I wrap each one around my ankle and finish a double knot when there is a knock. I crack the adjoining room door and several power bars and two juice bottles fly into my room, like a feeding at the zoo.

"Don't worry," I holler. "I'm full now. You're safe."

"Can't be too careful around wild animals," he says. "It doesn't look like rain, but bring your fleece jumper and wind breaker. The weather can change in a flash."

An image of dense fog around my kayak creeps in my mind, "Yeah, I get it."

I hitch up my day pack and remember one more thing from the morning, my most important item. "Don't worry," I call, as I pat my pant pocket. "I've got a compass, so we won't get lost." I don't think Uncle Teddy hears me, because he doesn't respond. The Dorkster, however, must have, because at that moment my phone dings and a blue light flashes. I squint at the screen. One new message from, guess who?

Knock, knock.

I text back - Who's there?

Banana.

Banana who?

Banana.

I sigh. *You've got to be kidding.* I twist to adjust my pack and another ding.

Knock, knock.

Who's there?

Banana.

Banana who?

Banana.

The Dorkster is bored, and I've become his cyber playmate. The phone dings again.

Knock, knock.

I text back—Who is this anyway?

Banana.

Heavy sigh—Banana who?

Banana.

"Are we ready to go?" Uncle Teddy hollers from his room.

I push his door open with my toe and walk in. "I'm being stalked." My fingers unsnarl a knot in my hair as I hold out my phone. "Loren is driving me nuts with text jokes."

Uncle Teddy laughs. "I forgot to tell you. I gave him a joke book before we left. Sorry."

My phone dings again, "Seriously?"

Knock, knock.

Okay, one more time—Who's there?

Orange.

I snigger. I know this one. Orange Who?

Orange you glad I didn't say banana.

Ha, ha, ha. I text back. Funny boy. Have fun.

Then I add—I'm totally bored and nothing happening. Love you.

That must have freaked him out, because I don't hear from him after that.

"Turn around," Uncle Teddy says, "I have something for you." Hoping for another cookie, but unsure, I turn my back to him. My shoulders jerk as he adjusts a couple of straps and pushes something into a mesh pocket. "Whatever you do, don't fire this thing," he says.

Chapter Nine

My hand reaches for the pocket and I feel a round bottle, like a water bottle. The cap has a loop, and I insert my finger and pull. Dangling from my index finger is a red can with the words, Bear Spray. I hold it up, like a dirty rag or something. "Fire this?"

"That's a highly concentrated form of pepper spray. I'll explain later, but whatever you do, don't pull the trigger guard off. We don't want any accidents."

My chin pulls back and I frown. "Is this safe to wear?"

He smiles. "You're good. Let's get going before it gets too late."

"That would be a shame," I say. "A real shame."

Loaded with extra clothes, rain coat, first aid kit, emergency supplies, and this strange red can, I drag myself down the hall. An agent stands near the elevator, feet apart and hands behind his back. He snaps to attention as we approach. The shaky elevator door opens as he checks the IDs hanging around our necks and nods us inside. On the first floor, another agent looks at them again as the door struggles closed. Finally, oh my gosh, yet another agent inspects our IDs at the front door as we leave the building. The warmth of the lobby and the constant monitoring by the agents makes me hyper aware and I begin to feel like a criminal as we step outside. A cloud drifts over the sun and casts a shadow that pulls my attention to the steep hills to the north. Again, a spider of fear crawls up my spine and I'm troubled, as if the mountain is watching me.

Uncle Teddy glances back and asks his favorite question, "Are you all right? You look white as a ghost."

I realize my arms are folded over my stomach and I'm hunched forward as if to hurl. "I'm fine," I say, faking a cough and standing upright, "something in my throat."

He watches me for a moment, then accepting my lie, turns left and heads down a gravel road past a small building where two agents, dressed in black suits, with machine guns over their shoulders, check our ID, a fourth time.

I roll my eyes and Uncle Teddy chuckles. "I guess they're prepared for the President and his guests. Can't be too careful."

I gently touch my belly and my fear settles.

"You'd think we're criminals. We're in the middle of nowhere," I say.

"Nowhere becomes somewhere when the President arrives," he answers and leads me to a steep hill. "Besides, this isn't nowhere, it's Glacier National Park. This is one of the few places in North America you can hike for an hour and be in wilderness, see glacial lakes, and walk on glaciers."

I roll my eyes.

"I know, it sounds like a lecture, but most likely, by the time you bring your children here, there won't be any glaciers."

Gravel crunches under my boots and a mother deer and her fawn raise their heads about fifty feet from me. "Look," I say. Before Uncle Teddy turns, they leap and are gone. "Two deer, they are so cute," I say and remember my thought. "I don't have children, and besides, why won't there be any glaciers?"

"Global Warming. We've talked about how the earth's warming caused changes in the waters around the San Juan Islands. It has the same effect here. Temperatures rise and, like at the polar caps, glaciers are melting. I don't know if lake levels are rising, but I do know they estimate by 2030, all glaciers in the park will be gone."

My right foot slips on the steep incline and I dig my poles into the moist, rich smelling dirt. I know a little about Global Warming. Simone told me how plant and marine life are being affected by the rising ocean temperatures.

"Some plants die, others become prolific and take over," she says. "This changes feeding grounds, kills some species of fish and allows others to thrive. As smaller fish die off, it means food isn't available for larger fish, and everything in the ocean is impacted."

She is so passionate about it, she almost cried when telling me. I didn't really get it. It seems like forever before it will affect me. But, when Uncle Teddy says all the glaciers will be gone by 2030, I think, that is like … soon.

Perspiration drips in my eyes and I gasp for each breath as we trudge up the summit of our first hill. My toe catches on a root and my hip lands on a blanket of pine needles. I roll and flop and face back down the trail. Expecting to see trees and brush, I'm not prepared for the beauty of the glacial valleys. After only thirty minutes, we are already hundreds of feet above the hotel and Swiftcurrent Lake. Three canyons reach out. Silver streaks of foaming water rush in each gorge. Sunlight sparkles off green and red rock walls rising up to jagged edged cliffs, towering like massive serrated knifes. The wind whistles through the trees and wood cracks as they sway. Cool and fresh, the air rushes around me. With each breath, I sense a tremendous presence—not an animal, something greater, something old and wise. I'm overwhelmed with a sense of my smallness. Through my hand, resting on the earth, there are vibrations. Although it's impossible, I'm sure it is ice scraping against earth, the carving out of another valley by the glaciers. I raise my hand to inspect tiny imprints in my palm from gravel. I press my hand to my cheek and whisper, "I'm sorry. I'm sorry we're losing you."

"Sammy, are …"

"Don't ask," I say, pushing myself up. "I'm fine."

"See those white spots," Uncle Teddy points.

I scrunch my eyes and raise my hand for shade. "No."

He nudges me with a pair of binoculars. Adjusting the viewer to my vision, I fine-tune the focus, and sweep the cliffs. Three birds circle a snow bank, and higher up are several white rocks. A rock moves. "Sheep," I yell, my hands shaking. I refocus and identify a furry white sheep."

"Close, actually a mountain goat, and a pretty big one," Uncle Teddy says.

Hundreds of feet above us, on a wall of stone, stands a mountain goat, beard dripping off his chin, he licks rocks. "How'd he get up there? He hardly has anything to stand on."

"Beats me. They're known for living at high altitudes and on pretty inhospitable environments. Amazing, huh?"

"Yeah, amazing. What's he eating?" The goat turns and faces me, as if he senses my gaze. His white beard sways from a tubular snout. Two curved black horns rise up from his forehead.

"He's probably licking lichen. It's supposed to have a high protein content."

"Lichen?"

"It's a composite organism that grows on rocks in the mountains, on trees, and in some desert environments. It's really two organisms, algae and fungus, that live in a symbiotic relationship and ..."

I cover my ears, "Okay, enough already—it's algae. The goat's totally amazing, like magic."

"That's not all," Uncle Teddy says. "There are bear, moose, elk, and a range of other wild animals in these woods. You've already seen deer and we will likely come across a few more on our hike."

"Bear?" I ask.

"Speaking of bear, I forgot to show you how to use your bear spray." He holds out a red can. I turn it in my hand. It has a white plastic slip lock at the top.

I grip the plastic cap. "Do you pull here?"

"Don't pull that," he gasps. "It keeps it from going off. It's super powerful pepper spray we can use as a last resort." When I didn't respond, he added, "If we're attacked by a bear."

Attacked by a bear. The idea never occurred to me. I imagine the energy of a bear would be like huge for sure. But sea lions and Orca whales are big too, and they don't threaten me. "Why would a bear attack me?"

He laughs. "I understand this doesn't compute since some of your best friends are wild animals. Even if it doesn't make much sense, bears are extremely dangerous. Not often, but sometimes, people are attacked. I'm just saying, if that happens, pull off the white cap, point the nozzle in the direction of the bear and fire. Then you're supposed to slowly back away. I'd probably run like the wind."

"Fire? Does it hurt them? I don't want to hurt them."

Uncle Teddy sighs. "Sammy, it won't hurt them, but it will stop them for a minute. While they're blinking, you have a chance to get away. You don't seem to understand. A bear won't care if you can hear their thoughts or not. They'll try to kill you. You will need to protect yourself. Just promise me you'll shoot."

I hear the irritation in his voice, the impatient anger that always rises up when we talk about my empathic sensitivity. Better to surrender than tell him the truth. "I understand. Bears are dangerous," I say. "I'll be careful, and I'll pull the trigger and back away or run or something." I pat the canister in an outside pocket of my backpack and scan the forest. *Don't worry, I won't hurt you.*

Two hours later, we trek along a dribbling stream, layered with flat rocks. The slabs create a natural stairway of one to two-foot-high steps that lead to a lake. My poles push at each oversized step until we reach a crest. I'd stared at my feet for so long I forgot where I was. My breath, fast and short, sweat dripping off my eyebrows, I lean on my poles.

"Here it is," Uncle Teddy says.

A breeze passes, the temperature drops then warms as if opening and closing a refrigerator door. The smells of pine and fir abruptly change to a piercing freshness that stings my nose and cheeks. Lifting my head, I almost fall off my poles. Forty feet below me, at the end of our trail, sits a small lagoon with real floating icebergs—like a mini Antarctica. *And I thought the Pacific Ocean was cold.*

Large stones, with several flat rocks perfect for sitting, form the edge of the lake. Uncle Teddy points to the ridge about five hundred feet above us and, with an adult's need to instruct, says, "This whole area used to be filled with a glacier. As the glacial ice melted and moved, it scratched out this bowl and the valley we just hiked through."

I nod, and remember the vibrations I felt in my hand.

"The lake formed about six thousand years ago when enough gravel and rock pushed up into a small dam. What's left is this very large pool of glacier water, and tiny icebergs." He gestures toward the walls and says, "A pair of your new goat friends."

Another gust of wind passes, cold and fresh off the lake, as we drop our packs and pick the perfect rock for a rest. I extend my leg, and push a small iceberg with the toe of my boot. My fingers brush the water. They turn blue. Between two large boulders, my back finds a flat spot and I let the sun thaw my hand.

Sandwiched between two boulders, I watch the mountain goats near the highest peaks around Iceberg Lake and I'm again filled with the ancient energy of an ice age over twenty thousand years old. Energy of the stones, some eight hundred million years old, moves in me. I sink into the ancient rock and it invites me to become part of the mountain. High above the two goats graze on sparse shoots of grass or lichen. I make a pillow with my arm and study the tiny white dots.

Something tingles and moves under my butt.

Chapter Ten

I bolt upright, and push off the rocks. A chipmunk darts between me and Uncle Teddy and disappears into a hole. Frigid moisture rises from the lake and my butt aches from sitting. "I'm ready when you are." I say. Stiff legged, I climb back to the trail. The afternoon sun warms my back as we hike back down the natural stairway. All I think of is lying down and my body submerged under the smooth white comforter at the lodge. Even the bed would feel soft now. The natural stone steps seem ten feet high and I lean on my poles to lower down each one, careful not to bend my cramping legs.

Thirty minutes along, Uncle Teddy stops at a sign that reads, Ptarmigan Lake and Tunnel. "Now the adventure begins," he announces with an enthusiastic grin.

"What? Begins? Aren't we heading back?"

"Oh no, it's still early. We have another ten miles."

"Ten miles? Are you kidding?" Poles dug in, I lean on them for support. My back twinges in agreement. He laughs and turns to head up another steep incline.

"I'm dying here," I say. He doesn't respond.

An hour later we hike around another small lake, no icebergs, to an almost vertical rocky incline. Panting like wild dogs, we stop for a drink. As I tip my water bottle up, a black hole near the upper edge of the hill catches my attention.

"What's that," I say between gargles.

"Ptarmigan Tunnel, a hole cut through solid rock. That's where we're headed."

Spit filled water streams from my mouth, and I study the cavern hundreds of feet above me. This time I see the glacial bowl cut in the mountains, and a saw-toothed ridge above it. The tunnel is cut near the top and connects either side of the ridge. A high pitch whistle pulls my attention. I turn just as a Golden Eagle lifts off a branch near the edge of the lake. It swoops down across the water, gold feathered wings sweep up as it snags a fish in fist size talons, and streaks away into the forest. Uncle Teddy stares away from me, so I catch my chance. "Lazy bones. I'll see you at the top," I say, and elbow past.

"Hold up, Sammy," he calls. "Time for a bathroom break."

I slow and glance around, "Bathroom break. Where?"

"Behind the rocks," he says with a smirk.

I raise my hand. "TMI. I'm not sticking around for that. I'll see you in the tunnel." The hike up to Ptarmigan Lake warms my muscles and I'm moving with ease. With each step my boots sink into loose gravel and my legs work to put distance between me and toilet man.

The tunnel entrance consists of a platform cut into the rock hill, with a steel frame around an opening, large enough for a person and a horse. Dead tired, I release my hiking poles and stand, arms spread, to let the cool breeze from the tunnel surround me. The temperature drops even more as I move from sunlight into darkness and the smell of animal dung rises up from the floor. I bend to pick up my poles; a gust of wind sweeps past the entrance behind me, and a whisper, as silent as salamander steps, creeps past. My head jerks and hits the rough stone wall.

No one in front of me, and no one behind—just the wind.

I rub the growing knob on my head and step near the center. Brightness at the other end blinds me until my vision adjusts. Craggy walls with sharp edges come into focus. The ceiling, of the same texture, has what appears to be hanging ornaments. Tiny, two inch bulbs hang from the entire upper part of the ceiling. I soon recognize the small pods, each attached by tiny feet and fingers pointed straight up, and heads pointed down. There are hundreds, maybe thousands, of bats. Liz pointed out similar species of bat that live on Orcas Island, so I am familiar with them. Many people are afraid of the magnificent creatures, but when they wake up, and scan the night air for flying insects, they are incredible. Their tiny bodies and scalloped wings let them dart left and right like fighter jets, even while their energy stays quiet and soft. Reassured, I walk forward, head low, feeling the uneven surface with my pole tips and the toes of my boots. I pass under them and their mouse like faces and black bug-eyes follow me.

"Are you alone?"

I scream and jerk. This time I'm sure it's a voice. A few bats flap their pterodactyl wings and squeal as they move away from me. Ahead I see the bright sun haloed around a black figure. I stand very still; my breath stops.

"You should not be up here alone."

"I have bats." *What a stupid thing to say!*

A soft, rhythmic, laughter reaches me.

"And my uncle is with me," I add.

"That is good," the voice says.

Something in the voice, or the voice's energy, assures me I'm safe and I take several steps forward as we talk. The adjustment of my vision and my nearness allows me to see a boy. He wears jeans, boots, a plaid shirt and a cowboy hat tilted back on his head. His thumbs are tucked inside his belt. His weight rests on one leg so his hip sticks out like a cow horn. His skinny frame makes him look tall.

"I'm sorry. Did I scare you?" he asks.

"No ... well ... yes, at first."

A smile flashes across his lips and his face rounds. From under his hat, long strands of black hair sweep back into a ponytail. Three lengths of leather, each with a feather fingered through the strands, hang down. He appears to be my age, but his skin is sun worn and his energy expands around me, merging with that of the ancient stone.

His hand extends toward me, "I am Runs with Fire."

I'm surprised to realize I'm close enough to touch him.

Did he mean he actually runs with fire or that is his name?

I smile, "Hi. I'm Sammy Carlisle."

Our hands touch and a tingle moves from my ribs around to the base of my spine. His hand feels warm and soft, almost like fur. Our eyes lock and a gold reflection in the shape of a diamond flashes in his black pupils.

"What tribe are you from?" he asks.

I pause. *That's a new one.*

"You are not Indian."

"No. I'm … I'm from the San Juan Islands. And you?"

"I am Blackfoot." His back straightens, and he stretches an inch taller. "I come from the Blackfoot Nation to the East."

He still holds my hand and I pull back.

"You are not like other white people." He says. My palm slips between his fingers.

I feel my shoulders shimmy and I'm suddenly cold. "What do you mean?"

"You carry spirit knowledge. It is very powerful."

"Spirit knowledge, what's that?"

"You speak with animals and beings that others cannot."

"How do you know that?" my curiosity peaked.

"I know because I too communicate with spirits."

Is he making fun of me?

"I don't know about speaking with spirits. Sometimes I think I hear animal's thoughts or sense their emotion. Is that what you mean?"

"Yes," he blinks with both eyes, and I feel, ever so slightly, a breeze from his peacock like eye lashes. "You should trust your instincts. You know and speak to animals. I watched you. You feel the bats, as I do. You are one with them."

"My friend, Simone, says I'm an empath."

"Empath? I do not know that word. What I know is my people, many lifetimes ago, were equal with everything in the Universe. We spoke with animals, rocks, trees and all things. We lived in harmony with nature. The Grandfathers tell us, 'One day our people let spirits turn our heads. We placed ourselves above other beings as better and special. In that moment, we separated from them, and lost our ability to communicate with most other things on this earth.'"

He shifts his weight to his other leg and his cow horn hip shifts to the other side. "Today, as some humans become balanced and equal, a few regain this ability. You have this special and very real sensitivity. Do not doubt yourself. Trust your intuition. Trust yourself." Once again his elegant eye lashes drop in a double blink.

"Sammy," Uncle Teddy calls from behind.

I turn as Uncle Teddy rushes toward me through the darkness.

"Are you okay?" he says, his boots scrape across the rocky floor.

"Okay? Yeah, I'm fine. Why?"

"That animal, what was it?"

"Animal? It's a boy—a Blackfoot Indian boy."

"Are you sure?"

"Of course I'm sure." My tone sharp with annoyance. "We were talking. He's nice."

Uncle Teddy pushes past and steps out of the tunnel. "So, where is he?"

"He's right …," I follow him into the bright glare of sunlight, and put on my sun glasses. "… here," I say, pointing to an empty trail. The path is wide enough for only one person, and cut along a sheer vertical wall that leads down to a valley and another lake a thousand feet below. Sparse bushes sprout up in patches of crusty dirt, while a few ground squirrels chirp from their dens. It seems impossible, but Runs with Fire vanished. My shoulders rise in confusion. "He was here a minute ago."

Uncle Teddy searches my face for an answer that might make sense, like I'm lying or something. "Well, whatever," he says with a sigh, "at least it wasn't a bear."

"Still worried about bears?"

"Yeah, especially over there behind the ..."

My hand shoots up, "Enough."

He looks toward the lake and laughs. "Right, we should get moving if we're going to reach Granite Park Chalet by late afternoon." I lift an eyebrow. "That's our halfway point," he says.

My butt pushes back. I bounce the pack on my hips, and tightened the waist belt. The trail to the valley winds below and I search for a plaid shirt or cowboy hat, but nothing. A shadow crawls up the mountain side while a cloud, a wisp really, sails above. White swirls spin in circles, and in it, I catch a glimpse of the Indian boy. He smiles; eyes wrinkled along the edges, warm and welcoming. His hair flows long and tangled. The cloud drifts, distorts, and elongates, then disappears as quickly as the boy himself.

What are you and where did you go?

Chapter Eleven

Like an insect with many legs, the Black Scorpions move through the dense brush of north Glacier National Park, known as Goat Haunt. Their objective is to pass through the Ptarmigan Tunnel to the mountains above Many Glacier Lodge. Nakale swings his hiking poles at waist high huckleberry bushes, mumbles, and curses, as they bush-whack through forested mountains, follow animal paths and avoid park trails.

"Bears love huckleberries," he mutters. "Why worry about being shot when we will probably be eaten anyway."

"Shut up," Fatuma whispers over her shoulder, "or I'll shoot you myself."

Ark raises his hand—a silent signal. Everyone stops except Nakale who, searching for bears and not paying attention, trips over Samuel's foot and into Ark.

"You stupid, freaking ..." Nakale yells, thinking it is Fatuma.

"Quiet," Ark hisses and pushes his hand against Nakale's face. Nakale's eyes widen as he looks past Ark at two hikers descending from the tunnel. Ark turns and nods to Samuel who jogs to Ark's side.

Arm stretched, Ark's crooked finger points south. "Why are they here?"

A man and a young woman descend from the tunnel. The woman appears to be searching for something.

Samuel shakes his head, "This should not be. The park is closed."

Ark checks his watch, "We're already late." He stares at Nakale with disgust, "Our mission cannot be compromised." His hand rests on Samuel's shoulder, as a father might console a son. "I know you asked me to avoid violence where possible, but this is unavoidable. To cut off the head of the Dragon, we must reach our goal today. This is our only chance." He glances at Samuel's rifle. "Take Nakale and neutralize them."

Samuel's face holds hard as granite. He learned as a child to mask his thoughts by controlling his emotions and wearing a blank stare. "I understand," he says, as his brain scrambles for an alternative option. "Maybe," he speaks with great caution, "if I approach the travelers alone, I can gain information that may benefit us."

Ark's tense vision bores into Samuel and searches for any weakness in his argument. With the slow cadence of a funeral march he says, "Yes, possibly. What do you suggest?"

"As you ordered," Samuel says, matching the measured manner of speech, "I will take care of the hikers, but before we do anything that might attract attention and ruin our mission, I will interrogate them—alone." Appealing to Ark's ego, he adds, "As you have instructed, we should take advantage of every opportunity."

Ark remains silent for a moment, "Yes, interrogate them. Learn more about the Dragon that might help us."

"Exactly," Samuel says with restraint, pleased that he may have averted violence. "If I hear anything that will help us, it is worth the risk."

"You are correct," Ark says. His palm caresses the stubble on his chin, and his eyes track the movement of the two hikers. "We must know as much as possible. I am glad I thought of this before you did anything rash. You are very smart, but only twenty, Samuel. Still, you are a loyal servant of our cause." He pats Samuel on the shoulder. "Do what you can." With a squeeze, he pulls Samuel forward. "But at the slightest sign of resistance, we agree, you will kill them."

"Of course," Samuel replies, letting Ark take credit for his idea and tipping his forehead away from Ark's putrid breath, "at the slightest resistance."

Samuel takes decisive steps to the back of the line. Fatuma follows each movement with admiration, while Nakale shuffles out of his way and watches with contempt. With two fingers, Samuel snaps open the chest strap on his pack and his large backpack slides silently onto a tree root. He leans his rifle on the pack, and secures it with a lanyard.

From his shoulder harness he removes a pistol and checks the clip—full.

With a slight dip of one knee and a childish grin, Fatuma holds out a fleece vest. "To keep you warm, monsieur, and cover your weapons." When Samuel does not respond, she continues, "What is your plan?"

"To circle around and advance from the south. I am just another adventurer lost in the woods." He slips his arms through the sleeve openings, adjusts the vest over his pistol, and zips. Resting his foot on a downed log, he lifts his right pant leg and secures a twelve-inch Israeli army knife to his calf. "How do I look," he asks, and jerks the vest down.

"Fantastic," Fatuma says. Her face moves close to Samuel's lips and her fingers spread evenly over his shoulders as she admires his well defined muscles and broad chest. She hands him two hiking poles, a red French beret, and a lightweight daypack with a few supplies. "This will make you the perfect innocent tourist, on the trail to Canada." She winks. "If they ask, say you slept under the tarp and planned for only one night on the trail. They'll think you are an idiot."

Nakale pounds dirt clods with the butt of his rifle as he glances from Ark to Samuel. He spits in the bushes, "Maybe a bear will get you," he says to himself.

Samuel smiles, nods once to Fatuma and makes a two-fingered salute to Ark. With urgent strides, he moves through the forest to circle around the two hikers. As Samuel passes, Ark touches his elbow and says, "Interrogate and exterminate."

Chapter Twelve

For an hour, we wind down the gravely trail. At first I check behind every bush for Runs with Fire, but by the time we reach the lower lake I'm so exhausted I forget about him. Sweat burns my eyes as we approach a wooden sign reading, "Granite Park Chalet—Four Miles." Below, hangs a picture of a red can with the words, "Bear Country—Carry Bear Spray."

"In all my years flying in the back country of Alaska," Uncle Teddy says, in an all too chirpy voice, "I've never gotten used to the idea that bears watch me," he pats the red canister hanging from his belt.

I wipe my nose and eyes on my shirt sleeve, "What do you mean, watch you?"

He glances back and laughs. "Watch, like look at me ... and you. What do you think they do while we walk by?"

"Eat Huckleberries? Eh Boo-Boo." I give my best cartoon imitation.

"Yes, eat berries because they don't have a leg bone to chew on. Trust me, when we walk by, they know we're here."

I glance around.

Huckleberry bushes and pine forest. A bear easily hides in those. But bears don't like leg bones, they like berries and fish—I hope. I'd know if a huge furry beast with energy like a woolly mammoth were around. I'd feel it.

"There aren't any bears around," I say. "Even if there were, they wouldn't be looking for us. They like berries and honey too much to come after us. I watch my cartoons, I know."

Uncle Teddy snorts, "Just in case, let's make some noise. The worst thing we can do is surprise a bear. Sing or clap your hands every once in a while, to let them know we're here." He claps his hands together and bellows something off key. When I don't join in, he continues even louder and more off key.

"Okay, okay, I give. I'll sing … There was a bear, in tennis shoes …"

I am so focused on trying to remember the old camp song, and navigating the uneven trail surface of broken stone and surface roots, I keep my eyes down.

"Umph," my head bumps into Uncle Teddy's backpack.

"What the …" I start to say, when he pushes his hand against my shoulder. I peek around—about thirty feet in front of us stands the woolly mammoth disguised as a gigantic grizzly. She sways left to right, and pulls huckleberry branches into her mouth, ripping an entire bush out of the ground. She notices us about the same time I see her. Her swaying stops.

"Stand behind me," Uncle Teddy says, "and get your spray out. I'll handle this." Uncle Teddy pushes me farther behind him and takes a step forward. Loose rocks give way, his foot slips, and he goes down like a sack of marbles. Exposed, I face the bear. Startled, she rises up on her hind legs and lets out a massive growl. A dank musky stench surrounds us and slobber covers the ground in front of her.

"Stay back," Uncle Teddy says as he struggles to rise up on one leg. The bear drops to all fours, the hair on her neck raises, and she rushes toward us. We both flinch and pull back. Uncle Teddy falls backward and I try to catch him. Quicker than a bear's breath, he lay at my feet, and I face the charging grizzly.

Liz told me bears sometimes fake an attack to scare their prey. Sure enough, instead of ripping us apart, the behemoth stops so close I can touch her nose, and I definitely smell her breath.

Drool drips from her lips and long fangs reach out from her massive mouth. Her body rocks and shifts weight from side to side. In the past month, I'd had many encounters with wild animals in the islands. Seals, sea lions and Orca whales have become my friends, even saved my life. Until now, however, none of them were bears.

"Drop to the ground, and cover your neck," Uncle Teddy says.

I can talk with her, I think, and I remember what the Indian Boy said, "Do not doubt yourself—trust your intuition—trust in yourself." I hear Uncle Teddy, but as she sways my body begins to move in rhythm with hers. I cock my head and we lock eyes. My body shakes as I whisper, "I'm not here to hurt you. Please don't hurt us."

She tilts her massive round head and blinks. With a loud roar, she focuses on Uncle Teddy.

"He's with me. Please, let us pass."

She raises her head and grunts, shooting snot on Uncle Teddy's pants. Her button-black eyes shift to me, and a soft mother like growl emerges. She rises up on her back legs and I blink, she blinks, and to my shock, shakes her head, turns, and stomps into the forest. The last image is of her gargantuan blond rump rumbling through the huckleberries, twisting trees, and she's gone.

We stay silent, in a moment of shock.

"What were you doing?" Uncle Teddy shouts. I jump. "One swing and your head roles down that trail."

I let out a nervous laugh. "No, it was okay."

"Okay? The heck it was. Sammy, you were three feet from a six-hundred-pound grizzly who would kill you with one swipe of her massive claws. She probably has cubs bigger than us." Uncle Teddy goes on, waving his arms, getting louder and louder, telling me I shouldn't trust wild animals and I should have had my bear spray out. I see he isn't in any mood for a discussion, so, even though I just communicated with the most ferocious animal I'd seen in my life, I nod my head in agreement and promise to never, ever, ever trust a bear again.

"No more bears," Uncle Teddy yells as he struggles to push himself up on his poles.

"No more dang bears."

Chapter Thirteen

I hold Uncle Teddy's arm to help him stand. He rises, loses balance, and jerks me down hard on my hip. To catch myself, I pull on his shoulder and he lurches back on the jagged rocks. He moans as I sit to get up, "I'm sorry," I say, "are you …"

"Bonjour," a voice sings to us from down the trail. "May I be of assistance?"

I spin around and roll on my stomach to identify the source of the dreamy voice. It's a man—a beautiful man. His smile flashes as he jogs toward us. My only thought, *he must use tooth whitener.* Reddish curls bounce out from under a red beret tilted to one side. I feel totally stupid and scramble to pull my feet under me.

"Are you all right, Mademoiselle? I hear him ask.

"Ahhh ..." I say, making every effort to sound intelligent.

"We're fine," Uncle Teddy interrupts, as he pushes himself up with his poles, a hint of anger in his voice. "And who are you?"

"Allow me," the curly head says. He places his hand under my arm and I lift to my feet. For a moment, I'm floating.

"I am Samuel Bonaparte," he says with a slight bow, "and to whom do I owe the pleasure?"

"Sammy ... Samantha," I stammer, trying not to stare into his huge brown eyes.

"Sammy Samantha? That is a very interesting name, and a coincidence."

I start to explain when Uncle Teddy pushes his hand forward. "I'm Ted Crenshaw." He steps between me and Samuel. "Pleased to meet you."

"The honor is mine. Are you all right?" Samuel Bonaparte asks, surveying Uncle Teddy's leg.

"Yes, we're fine, just a small accident on the rocks."

Samuel slides his day pack off and pulls out a red bag marked with a white cross. "Can't be too careful," he says through a glistening smile. "I'm told the park is filled with bears." From a side zipper, he removes a small round compact.

"We have our first aid kit," Uncle Teddy insists.

"But do you have Arnica? This will help heal any muscles or tendons that may be damaged. Please, take it. It is a natural salve that speeds healing."

Uncle Teddy frowns, but accepts the box. He inspects the label from all angles, smells the gel, and finally sits to remove his hiking boots. "You have quite a famous name."

Samuel laughs, "Yes, Napoleon, a distant relative. No fame associated with it these days."

"Napoleon?" I ask.

"Yes, a former French Emperor of some repute. The most it's worth these days is an occasional free glass of wine."

As Uncle Teddy spreads the salve over his ankles and calves, I notice him study Samuel and his open backpack.

"What brings you to Glacier?" Uncle Teddy asks.

"I'm hiking from Two Medicine in the south, through Goat Haunt, to Canada," Samuel answers, equally curious about our packs. Samuel and Uncle Teddy continue to ask and answer questions. It is like watching a chess game, Uncle Teddy asks and answers, to learn more about Samuel, and Samuel does the same. Both act calm and distracted. "Where are you from? Why are you here? Can I help you to your destination?" Uncle Teddy is careful in his answers not to give away our reason for being in Glacier, but I'm not as quick. They're conversation excludes me, and after a while my blood boils. *I saw him first.*

"My name is really Sammy Carlisle." I interrupt. "We're only here for three days. The President's conference ends day after tomorrow."

With the word, "President," they both spin to face me and go silent. Uncle Teddy's eyes widen to the size of tennis balls; Samuel stares down and adjusts his vest.

"My university," Uncle Teddy stutters. "I flew us here for a class reunion, nothing of importance." Samuel nods as if he understands. I let out a long sigh and struggle to think of something to say.

"And you?" Uncle Teddy hands Samuel the Arnica, "You are Canadian?"

Creases form between Samuel's eyebrows. He wets his lips, "Yes, from Quebec, eh?" They both chuckle and his smile reappears. "On picking up my backcountry permit, I was told to complete my trek by today. My misdirection caused a delay. Still, if I hurry, I should be out of the park by nightfall." He pushes the first aid kit back in his pack, and glances at me. Butterflies leap in my stomach and I search the ground to avoid his stare.

He follows my gaze to a trickle of water crossing the trail. "I see you must cross a small stream," he says. With that, he removes a plastic tarp from an outside pocket, and spins it above his head like a matador. It spreads out in a square. With an elegant bow, he lays it over the stream. My cheeks burn like hot rocks when his eyes focus on me.

"Mademoiselle Sammy, a pretty woman should not dirty her slippers, even if they have seven eyelets and lug soles."

My hiking boots are covered with mud and fir needles. I look like a logger. "Slippers?"

"Cyrano de Bergerac at your service."

The sun peeks out from behind clouds, birds sing, and in that moment, my boots feel like slippers. I giggle. Uncle Teddy's eyes roll.

"Are you familiar with Cyrano?" Samuel asks.

My mind races as I step forward. I have visions of searching my computer—the screen blank. "I've heard of him ... I think."

"Cyrano was an unattractive man with a curiously long nose, who loved a beautiful young woman—Roxanne. I've heard, as a gentlemanly soldier, he sacrificed his cloak to protect her slippers. More importantly, he wrote love letters for another more attractive man who also loved her, but was too shy to reveal his affection. Without realizing it, the beautiful Roxanne fell in love with the man who wrote the letters—Cyrano."

I glance over and see Uncle Teddy's face tighten, his eyes narrow. He reminds me of a wolf ready to attack.

Caught up in the roll playing, I blurt out, "But you're not unattractive and I know who you are."

When I say, "know who you are," we all freeze. Samuel glances from me to Uncle Teddy. For a moment, a cloud passes over, but the sun returns when he takes my hand.

"Of course," he says, "allow me to assist you across the stream." His fingers touch mine. My skin prickles, and heat rises in my chest. I'm dizzy with his attention, as he guides me through the puddle. I stumble, splash mud on his legs, and fall into his arms. We face each other, for just a blink, and I fall into the pools of his dark chocolate eyes. Just as quick, we both let go.

"Thank you," I say and leap over. He reaches for Uncle Teddy's arm.

"I'm fine," Uncle Teddy yanks his arm back and sloshes through the steam a few feet from the tarp, kicking water with each step. "We have to go."

"Yes, it is getting late." Samuel shakes the tarp. "Are you leaving soon," he asks.

"Yes, tonight," Uncle Teddy lies.

"That is good." Samuel locks eyes with me, and instead of a smile I receive a cold, ice hard stare. "The forest can be a very dangerous place," he says. "Please take care of yourselves." He wraps the tarp over his arm, as if it were a fine silk shawl, bows deeply, and with a smirk, winks at me. My head spins.

"Until we meet again. Au revoir." He twirls his cap, slides it over his bouncing curls and saunters up the trail. For the first time, I notice his cute butt.

"Oh for gosh sakes," Uncle Teddy says, with disgust.

"Oh my gosh," I agree, with delight.

Chapter Fourteen

C hocolate Eyes disappears in the forest behind us as we head up the steep trail to Granite Park Chalet. I lean hard on my hiking poles to keep pace with Uncle Teddy who marches ahead not saying a word. I'm not sure what has happened. I only remember Samuel looked at me and winked—my head exploded when he called me pretty. I don't remember anyone ever telling me that before, except my Mom. This is completely different. I'd read about love and seen it on the Internet, but to feel it. I'm not even sure I should call it love, just that he is so beautiful.

"We've got a long way to go," Uncle Teddy interrupts my thoughts. He pushes forward, his head down—energy scratchy and rough.

My empathic sensitivity began as a child. The first time I remember using it I was about four. I sensed something wrong and went outside to find a small injured bird on our porch. Mom put it in a shoe box and we nursed it. When ready, we let it go. As more incidence of my being called by animals occurred, she recognized what she termed my special sensitivity. Dad thought I acted out to get attention, but my sensitivity strengthened, until now I sense some people's energy as well as animals. Uncle Teddy's energy scratches against me like sandpaper.

"Are you angry?" I ask.

He turns on me and drops forward on his hiking poles. "Yes, I'm angry," he yells. "That guy flirted with you, and the incident with the bear, it really concerns me. Everything is getting out of control."

"Out of control? No," I say. "Everything's fine. He was being nice. Besides, he's a man. He can't flirt with me. I'm a kid."

"Don't fool yourself, Sammy. Men flirt with pretty young women to get what they want."

I almost fall over. "You think I'm pretty?"

"Yes, of course I think you're pretty."

"No," I press. "I mean pretty like someone other than you would like me."

"Yes ... No," he stammered. "What I mean is yes, you're very pretty and I don't like some jerk approaching you like that. And his stupid red hat, I'll knock it off if he tries that again."

A smile creeps across my face as I stare off into leaf-green trees, almost expecting, hoping, to see Samuel. I remember his hair flowing out from under his cute beret. I feel Uncle Teddy's eyes bore into me, and I straighten up like a wooden soldier. "Of course, stupid hat, I understand. I get it."

"We'll talk more about this later," he says, "but for now, we need to be moving." He turns and, as he climbs up the steep hill, I notice his limp is almost gone.

The trail takes us through a low growth forest of Aspen and Pine trees. The higher we climb, the shorter the trees. I let my hand slip across the smooth white bark of the Aspen, and imagine what it would be like to touch Samuel's cheek. Grass brushes my palm and I see his hair between my fingers. *He flirted with me—that is so totally awesome.*

Before I know it, we reach the summit at the Chalet. The building, made of stone with two small windows facing us, appears empty with no one around. We pass, as the sun sets across a pink and orange, pencil thin horizon. Marshmallow clouds float above the towering peaks of Montana's Rocky Mountain range. Runs with Fire sneaks into my mind—another unusual young man—that makes two in one day. As I think of the Indian boy, I realize his energy still surrounds me. Trust yourself, he'd said, and I did. Uncle Teddy was frightened and angry when I stepped forward, but the bear understood—I know she heard me.

"Sammy, stop." Uncle Teddy shouts. My boot skids and I sit hard. The trail has turned to chunky rock that pokes my butt. My right heel presses into a crack in the stone, and my left foot dangles out over … out over nothing. I scoot back and lean so I peek over the edge. A cliff falls below me for what seems like miles. My stomach leaps into my throat, "Oh my gosh, I gasp. Where are we?"

"We're at the top of Swift Current Pass. Are you okay?"

"Yeah," I roll over on my stomach and glance up—*no Samuel.* "I'm fine, but where do we go from here?"

"Down," he points to the cliff face, "twenty-five hundred feet to the valley, then another two miles to the lodge."

"Twenty-five hundred feet? Down?"

The path switches back and forth down the face of the mountain. We move close to a waterfall that streams over a smooth rock face and free falls to the bottom. Misty spray washes across my face; my nose twitches. After the long hike, and the heat of the day, the icy shower gives me a shot of energy. Shortly after, a breeze comes up, and a cold wave rolls through me.

Eyes focused on the trail, I don't notice it getting dark, so much so that I'm hardly able to see my yellow shoe laces in front of me. I raise my eyes and a flash blinds me.

"I'm sorry," Uncle Teddy says as he hands me a small bundle of straps, "Here's a headlamp. We'll need these to stay on track."

I pull one end and it unfolds into a lamp with an adjustable strap. I push a button and I'm staring right at the light again. For two minutes I see blinking bubbles pop around me. I slip it over my head. The spotlight rotates around me as I turn my head—*awesome.* Uncle Teddy is right. We need the lights more than ever.

We creep along a one foot wide path for what seems like hours. About half way down, the path narrows and gets steeper. In places, it's washed out and literally disappears. Uncle Teddy steps forward to a section where the trail has collapsed. "The best way to cross is to push down hard in the scree to make a step."

"Scree?"

"The loose gravel. Shift your weight slowly, to be sure it will hold," he takes a stride, "then lean and push your other foot down to move forward." Using his poles to balance, he tromps across a near vertical twenty-foot section.

On the far side, he waves to me. I feel the blood drain from my face, and I stand glued to the mountain. He waves again and finally says, "Your turn. You can do it."

White as a mountain goat, I stand measuring what feels like a ten-thousand-foot long gap with no trail. I know … I really know … I'm gonna to die. My arms and legs shake and my scalp prickles like I'm wearing a hat with a thousand needles, but I don't want him to know my fear. With eyes closed and hardly able to move, I plant my poles, raise my hand to my neck, and finger the locket Mom gave me when she was sick. I open it and her face, next to mine, stares at me. Her words come to me, "You are courageous, strong and beautiful. Don't let anyone take that away from you." I gulp and whisper, "Mountain, you won't take that away from me." I make one step forward, stamp my boot and shift my weight. The loose scree gives way, but my foot holds. I take another step, slip and hold, and then another, and another. In minutes, which I'm sure is really hours, I cross the washout to the solid trail again. Uncle Teddy takes my arm. "Thanks," I say, to both him and Mom.

Over the next mile we cross three more slide areas that seem progressively longer and scarier, before we finally reach the bottom. As we move into the valley, heat rises from the rocks and the sweet smell of huckleberry surrounds us. Uncle Teddy lags behind, but our pace is steady.

I slow as a rush of energy pulses through me. I can't see anything, but I taste its presence. The force pushes against me from my left side, near a grove of white pompoms. I start to say something, but realize Uncle Teddy won't understand. Remembering my earlier words to the bear, I repeat them several times.

I'm not here to hurt you. I am your friend.

We move forward and the energy rises up, like a mountain above me, pushing down, suffocating me. I choke and cough, my legs weaken and I stumble. Unable to move, I'm about to call for Uncle Teddy when something crashes on my left, tree branches whip past, and small Aspen bend and break. Hoofs and dirt fly up as a bull moose plows through the forest in front of me, heading to the lake on our right.

"Sammy," Uncle Teddy screams, "are you all right?"

I can't speak for a minute, but I realize if I hadn't stopped, five feet further along on the trail, I would have been crushed. "I'm okay," I say looking into the forest, "and thank you."

"I didn't do anything."

"Yeah, I know, but thank you anyway." This time I'm not sure who I'm speaking to.

After that, I talk to the energy that follows me. Although I can't know for sure, I'm confident it's the bear.

"We're just here hiking. You wouldn't believe the day I've had ... and the boys I've met. One turns into clouds. Seriously, just floats away. The other, wow, the other has eyes that you could swim in."

I explain all the strange things that had happened and soon lose track of time and distance. My eyes focus on the white circle of light that spots a small portion of the trail in front of me as I stumble and mumble along.

"What did you say?"

I glance up. Beyond Uncle Teddy's shadowy silhouette, lights from the lodge reflect off the lake. A rush of warmth lifts to my cheeks as I realize I've been talking to that bear for the last two miles of the hike. "Nothing, just practicing what to say to the President."

"Right, the President. I almost forgot." He glances at his watch. "It's after nine. Are you hungry?"

My stomach growls a ferocious response, "Now that you mention it, I'm starving."

He smiles, "Come on, we're almost there."

My feet move in silent automation chasing the moving light. My toes ache with each step and my poles feel like survival tools. Despite my exhaustion, a new kind of energy runs through my veins. I'll never see either of them again, but today I met two exciting people from entirely new places.

Even if I don't meet the President, this is a real adventure. Uncle Teddy is right; Glacier is amazing.

At the lodge a starched, scowl faced, Secret Service woman checks our IDs. She announces our arrival into her radio, a scratchy voice responds and she leans open the door. The cold stainless steel counters sit empty, as is the kitchen. We search two humongous refers and snatch some bread, cheese, meat, and two small cartons of milk. "This must be meant for us," he says. His eyebrows move up and down like crawling caterpillars as he holds out a plate with half a chocolate cheese cake.

"Definitely for us," I agree.

"Peaceful," Uncle Teddy says as we walk through the silent basement. I touch my scab and carefully avoid the walls. Behind another agent, the antique elevator doors open and close like a cavernous jaw. Two floors up, we stop at another checkpoint and drag our feet to our rooms. My legs ache and my butt throbs from a seriously too long day.

"Yeah ... peaceful," I say, in a delayed response. "See you tomorrow."

My door snaps shut and I turn the lock. Sandwich fixings sit on the nightstand as I struggle with my boots and toss my clothes across the room. The last thing I see is the chocolate cheese cake and all I'm aware of is my head pushing into the pillow ... and those huge dark chocolate eyes.

Chapter Fifteen

Samuel moves rapidly north until well out of sight. He smiles, satisfied at the irritation he caused the man, Ted, and the look of complete surprise on Sammy's face when he twirled his poncho and laid it over the trickling stream. Ready to laugh out loud, he feels a hand slap on his arm, "You had fun?"

Samuel, smile gone, turns to face Ark. Fatuma scowls at him. "Fun?" Samuel asks.

"Yes, I saw how you pandered to that woman," Ark says.

Samuel remembers Ark's command to interrogate and exterminate. "She's a child. I simply wanted her to trust me."

"She didn't look like a child to me," Fatuma says with a knife sharp edge to her voice.

"Quiet," Ark orders over his shoulder. Fatuma takes one step back. Nakale, some feet away, crouches as if to hug his stomach. "What did you learn?" Ark says.

"He's just a delivery boy for the retreat," Samuel says, shifting his gaze from Fatuma to Ark. "He brought his niece along for the trip, to deliver fish or something. They lied about this being a university gathering, but that's to be expected. They are of no danger to us."

Ark's eyes focus over Samuel's shoulder down the trail, as if dreaming of his future. "That is for me to decide." The lids of his eyes wrinkle, "I told you to kill them. Why did you disobey me?"

Not prepared, Samuel searches his memory and finds the word, pilot.

"Pilot," he says. "He let slip he is a pilot."

Ark's eyebrow snakes up in a devilish grin.

"I thought an alternate escape route might come in handy," Samuel adds, relieved he found a reasonable response.

"Yes." Ark shifts his pack and raises his crooked finger to the mole on the side of his nose, fingering it in thought. "That may be handy. You did well Samuel ... very well."

Fearing Ark's explosive anger, Nakale inches his way out of the bushes toward the trail, and unintentionally into Ark's vision.

"Wait, we cannot use the trail. It is too exposed," Ark orders.

Nakale's body jerks then slumps. He swears under his breath, "There are bears."

Never missing an opportunity, Fatuma growls through her teeth, "Grrrr."

"The path is too exposed," Ark says again, as he runs his fingers over a map. He squints, "We must follow this stream back north, then this ridge to the east. There are no trails and we will remain unnoticed. With luck, we will approach the cliffs just north of the lodge by nightfall.

Nakale's eyes dilate in horror, "Cliffs?"

Fatuma pokes her finger toward him, "Not so worried about bears now, huh?"

"Shut up," Nakale bellows. Fatuma covers her face and shrieks with laughter.

The arguing, like children in the backseat of a long drive, triggers Ark's anger. He releases his pack and allows it to fall to the ground. Fatuma and Nakale take a step away and go silent.

"Scout ahead along the ridge." Ark orders. "Find us a point above the lodge where we can camp for the night. Samuel and I will bring your backpacks with us."

Eager to avoid Ark's fury, Fatuma and Nakale drop their packs and, to the sounds of boot steps and cracking branches, hurry through the forest.

Samuel surveys the four packs at their feet. "Is getting rid of them worth our carrying their loads?"

"Anything is worth not listening to their bickering," Ark says as he hoists one seventy-pound bag, then his own. "Either that, or I might kill them myself."

Nakale, upset that he is assigned to being a scout, consoles himself with the fact that Ark will carry his pack. As always, he does not protest to Ark, but complains to Fatuma from the moment they leave. "I do not know why I am always assigned to do the dirty work," he says. "I'm the most experienced, and I'm treated like a child," he continues. "I deserve better. I ..."

Fatuma ignores him and pushes forward in the lead. She turns right at a large pine tree and Nakale complains she turned too early. Farther on, when Fatuma turns right again, saying it is east, Nakale argues it is north. As the trail tracks up a steep hill, Nakale slips and protests it is too hard. Finally, when they reach an outcropping a thousand feet above the lodge, he grumbles the cliff is unclimbable, saying, "There is access from the east and no need to drop down this deadly rock face."

"You are such a coward," Fatuma taunts as she steps to the edge. "A strong Nigerian boy like you shouldn't be afraid of rappelling a few hundred feet, and scaling down a little hill."

"Little hill?" Nakale says. "The face is thousands of feet high. One slip and we die."

Her fists plant firmly on her hips, "Think like a mountain goat," Fatuma says, as she gazes down on small twinkles of yellow light beaming through the lodge windows. A shadow moves beyond one window and she imagines following it through the sight of her rifle. "Besides," she continues, "if you keep whining, Ark will break you like a twig. Personally, I think the mountain is safer." She steps away. "Come, let us find Ark and Samuel."

"What? I don't want to go back," Nakale protests. "Ark said they would carry our packs. Fatuma, wait."

Spruce and fir branches whip behind Fatuma, who moves at a pace she hopes might leave Nakale behind. Still complaining, damp needles slap against Nakale's arms and face as a three-quarter moon throws spirit shadows around him. Ark and Samuel have progressed half way under the burden of double packs. Samuel stops, "Hear that?" he whispers.

"The trees," Ark says and they slip behind standing tree trunks for camouflage.

Sensing an unusual silence, Fatuma wets her lips and gives three short whistles. Samuel responds with one long whistle. An owl hoo's in the distance. Shortly after, Nakale bursts through a stand of bushes, stumbles, and lands at Fatuma's feet. She puts her finger to her lips, pats him on the head, and whispers, "A shame, I thought I'd lost you." Nakale slaps her hand away, and rises as Ark steps between them.

"Report," Ark orders.

Before Nakale can complain, Fatuma machine guns her plan, "As you said, the face is an easy rappel to the lower hill. We can approach on foot from there. I suggest we camp on the cliff tonight, and be ready to scale the face before sunrise."

"It's impossible," Nakale argues. "The trail from the east is safer and easier."

Ark pushes Nakale away. "We approach down the face of the cliff in the morning. Guards will watch the easier routes, and no one will suspect an approach from such a deadly precipice." He turns on Nakale, pointing with his nose. "You are not afraid, are you?"

"No sir," Nakale responds too quickly. Already he has thoughts of desertion. It is better to live in fear, he reasons, than to be a dead terrorist.

Chapter Sixteen

A misty glow above the plains to the east pushes against the still dark sky. Gravel crunches under quick moving combat boots. A rough hand shakes Nakale's shoulder. "Get up. We're late."

Samuel watches Ark rouse Nakale, adjusts his pack, and checks his ropes. Stiff from the night's sleep on glacial rock, Fatuma stretches, inspects her climber's cable, and fingers through a row of oval carabiner clips to ensure they function properly. Nakale sits up as a helicopter passes overhead. The group scatters to the cover of nearby bushes. He doesn't move, but pulls his sleeping bag up and peeks out like a mole.

"Don't worry," Samuel whispers as the propellers whip past, "they are landing with a few of the delegates. They are not looking for anything in the dark."

"Samuel," Ark says as he scans the cliff face, "you and Nakale pair up. I will go with Fatuma. We must start the decent of the cliff face now before the morning light exposes us."

Nakale peeks out from his bag. "Are you sure about this?"

Samuel laughs. "Nothing to it. You and I will work together, rappelling down the face to ledges about every one hundred fifty feet."

Nakale's eyes widen as he peers over the edge. "And what if we miss a ledge?"

"Won't happen," Samuel assures him. "I'll go first. Then you lower our packs. I'll secure them and you rappel down. We'll reposition the ropes and I'll go first again. It's about a thousand feet, so we'll do that six times to reach the hill at the bottom."

Samuel pulls the backpacks to the edge, and with a sound-deadening plastic mallet, pounds a spike into the rock face. Next to him, Ark pounds a spike and motions to Fatuma to be ready. Samuel threads a rope through a carabiner on the spike and attaches it to his pack. He repeats the process, and connects a second rope to his climbing harness. While Nakale scrambles to close his pack, Samuel grips the lanyard, steps to the edge, and leans backward until he lies horizontal in the air with his feet pushing against the cliff wall.

"When I reach the first ledge, I will signal you with my red flashlight pointed straight up, so it won't be seen from below. You lower the backpacks, and rappel down." Samuel relaxes his grip. "See you below."

The smooth round line slips between his hands as he steps backward down the face of the mountain. In eight minutes, he reaches the first ledge. With his military flashlight he blinks three times.

Expecting the packs to come crashing down, Samuel is amazed when Nakale does exactly as he is asked and is soon standing on the ledge with the two backpacks. Samuel slaps him on the shoulder.

"You're a good man, Nakale. I knew you could do it."

Nakale's impulse is to grumble, but he smiles. He likes the compliment and is excited about demonstrating his worth. "If we hurry, we can beat them," he says, nodding toward Fatuma and Ark, who reach their first ledge. "Let me go first."

Samuel hesitates, before he can respond, Nakale grabs the rope and clips onto the next carabiner. Excited, he walks backwards, and steps off the ledge. In the first fifty feet he trips twice and once spins in mid-air before regaining his footing. Samuel winces, but waves when Nakale gives him a thumbs up. In the next one hundred feet, he trips and falls to his side several times, but, to Samuel's amazement, Nakale rappels the sheer wall to the second ledge. He signals Samuel and receives the packs. As soon as Samuel's feet touch the second ledge, Nakale eagerly steps backward and descends the next segment. As if having practiced the routine many times, together, they descend the cliff wall in less than forty minutes.

On the last drop, Nakale goes first and Samuel lowers their bags to the bottom. As the bags drop the last few feet, Nakale blinks his flashlight wildly encouraging Samuel to hurry. Samuel glances to the side and sees Fatuma begin her final descent. He leans back, plants his feet and instead of slowly releasing the rope, he allows it to rip through his grip. His palms grow hot and the cable wears holes in his leather gloves. Fatuma runs backward, equally fast. As she readies to pass Samuel she lets out a cackling laugh. He realizes she is moving faster than him, and with forty feet left and determined to beat her, he lets go of the rope. In a moment, his speed accelerates to a free fall. Air explodes in his ears and he is slightly disoriented until he feels his boot kick a finger like rock extending from the face. Samuel pushes, performs a perfect backward summersault, and lands like a cat. He turns and bows as Fatuma catches her heel, and lands on her backside with a thud. Nakale, ecstatic, performs a silent celebratory dance, while Fatuma gathers herself and marches toward him, eyes flashing anger.

"Quiet," Ark's gravelly whisper brakes the moment. Nakale presses his hands to his stomach and mimes a silent belly laugh, while another chopper whirs overhead. From the safety of a vertical crevasse in the wall, Ark watches the helicopter land at the lodge. He waves to his troops. "Stow the ropes and climbing gear in here," he orders. As Nakale approaches, a few supply boxes drop from his pack, and Ark notices a rip through which supplies have fallen out. With uncontrollable instinct, Ark swings, raking his large hand across Nakale's face. "You are a horse's ass," he roars. "I should get rid of you, now."

Blood oozes from Nakale's cheek and he goes down. Memories of beatings from his captors when he was a child soldier fill his thoughts. He pushes up and stands. His legs move in a short, erratic jig he invented to avoid showing pain.

Realizing Nakale's torment, Samuel rushes between the two men. "He's done well and we need him to complete our mission," Samuel says. "We were quick because of Nakale. Let's not let anger dictate our actions."

Ark spits and turns on Samuel. Their eyes fix and Samuel remembers his own father, a man who beat his son and nearly killed his wife. Ark has the same kind of eyes that jerk in random motion, and hands that spasm out of control.

"This isn't a game," Ark shrieks. "Keep him out of my way."

Samuel steps back, flinches, and nods. Ark's rage triggers a childhood response. "Yes sir," Samuel says. His mind whirls with a new awareness. How could he have missed it? He's seen Ark's anger before, but never to this degree. Now he knows, it's obvious, Ark is as crazy as his own father was.

Tiny gravel avalanches stream down the hillside as Ark stomps back and forth to survey their situation. What he sees is the hotel below, the lake to the right, and a river rushing over a small dam to the left. Ark identifies Angie on the water's edge and makes a mental note that the plane is their possible escape vehicle. In the parking lot, in front of the hotel, he sees a helicopter idling on the landing pad—another possible escape tool. To its right, near a road, sits a shack with two guards.

He takes a deep breath. "The President," he mumbles to himself, "is inside. He will soon learn how deadly a Scorpion's sting can be."

Chapter Seventeen

A knock shakes the door. "Go away," I yell. Again, a knock, "I already told you, I'm not buying." *Uncle Teddy has such bad timing.*

I raise my head from the sink and rub my hair. Water drips over my shoulders and down my back. The hotel soap is some kind of environmental, recycled, reusable, nontoxic, biodegradable product that says it's made of papaya, avocado, eucalyptus, cannabis, and coconut oil. I have no idea if that's good for you, but I like the "no animal testing" statement, and it smells good and makes my hair shiny. The door vibrates under three more thumps. I wrap a dry towel around my head and stomp to the door, "All right, but you should know I don't want what you're selling." I tighten my robe and yank the door open. "What?"

"Miss Carlisle?" A tall, slim, man says. He is dressed in a dark blue suit and red tie, and wears a tiny American flag pin on his lapel. The corners of his mouth crinkle in a slight smile.

"Oh, yes she is, I mean yes I am, Mr. President," I pull the robe tighter and adjust my turban.

"I assure you, I'm not selling anything. I wanted to introduce myself and ask if you need anything." His slight smile expands to a grin.

"Yes sir, I know. I didn't know before, but if I'd known it was you I would have known. You know what I mean?"

He chuckles, "Yes, I think I understand. May I address you as Samantha?"

"Oh yes. Please, call me anything you like. And ... I'll call you ... ah ... Mr. President?"

His laughter fills the corridor. As my back muscles relax, I realize I've been standing like a toy soldier.

"Yes, that is what most people call me. It's a big day. We will be meeting most of the morning in closed session. Your introduction will come right after lunch."

I nod and catch my headdress as it slips and flops over my left ear.

"It won't be much," he continues, "just a few words about your connection with animals and your heroics back home. I've been accused of being a little long winded, but I'll try not to embarrass you."

Heat rises in my cheeks and I shuffle my feet. "I'm sure that's fine. But wait, do I need to say anything?"

"No, not unless you want to?"

I shake my head.

"Have you been treated well?"

"No. I mean I don't want to speak, and yes, they're treating me great, thank you."

The President peeks over my shoulder. "Looks like they gave you a room similar to mine—early American, don't you think?

I scramble for a brilliant response when Uncle Teddy approaches from the hall. He stands at attention a couple of feet away and clears his throat. I'm saved when the President turns.

"Mr. President, I'm Samantha's uncle, Ted Crenshaw."

The President offers his hand. "Mr. Crenshaw, it's a pleasure to meet you. Navy pilot if I'm not mistaken."

Uncle Teddy's eyebrows worm up in surprise. "Yes sir, that's correct, Second Gulf War."

"Second. We're grateful for your service." He turns to me, "Your father served in Operation Desert Storm. Is he here?"

My mouth goes dry. I search for an answer and finally stammer, "Yes and no, I mean …

"Yes sir," Uncle Teddy interrupts. "He did serve, but he's not here. I regret to say, he's not doing well."

The president raises his hand to his cheek and glances from Uncle Teddy to me, "I'm so sorry to hear that."

I pull the lapels of my robe, wishing we weren't having this conversation.

"PTSD, sir, he's had a tough time lately." Uncle Teddy pauses and peeks at me. "He's now homeless."

The President's eyes narrow and his forehead creases. Hands clinched, he bows his head for a moment. "I deeply regret hearing that. Our veterans deserve all we can do for them." He looks directly at me, as if reaching out with his eyes, "This must be very difficult for you, Samantha."

I glance away. It's all I can do to hold it together.

"I'll see what I can do, I promise."

For some reason, I know he means it. He glances at the black suit standing next to him, who nods in response.

"An escort will be at your room about noon to pick you both up. I look forward to seeing you then." As he starts to leave, I remember the gift.

"Mr. President," I blurt. "May I give you a small present from home?"

The President glances at the agent and smiles. "I think that will be all right, under the circumstances."

The officer accepts the long, flat box Uncle Teddy gave me earlier. "Thank you Samantha," the President says. "I'll meet you in a while."

"Thank you Mr. President." I step back. "I'll be out in a while," I say to Uncle Teddy and close the door. As soon as the door shuts, my chest heaves, and tears begin. I hadn't thought about Dad for several days, and wasn't ready for the grief. But grief doesn't wait for ready. I stumble to the bed and bury my face in the comforter. "Get well," I sob. "Why can't you just get well?"

Chapter Eighteen

I don't move for an hour. All I think about is Dad, afraid and alone. He and Mom separated over a year ago, and I never knew why until Uncle Teddy explained Dad was a hero in the Gulf War and came home sick with Post Traumatic Stress Disorder. It's a mental illness, he explained, that is the result of the trauma people experience in war or other extreme situations. At first it just pissed me off even more, that he would get sick like that and use it as an excuse to leave us. I searched on line and found out that people can't help it. It's like a second person living inside of them, taking over their thoughts and body like a zombie attack. In some cases, they just withdraw, go inside themselves and do anything—drugs, alcohol, anger, violence—anything to make the fear and memories go away. That's why Dad drinks and why he left us. Now he lives in a shelter in Portland, or, I guess, on the streets. Half of me wants to help him, the other half hates him. All the time, I miss him. And the

President, saying he wants to help. It sounded good at first, but that's BS. He should already be helping.

A knock on the door shakes me out of my angry state. "Sammy," Uncle Teddy's voice comes from the adjoining room. "Are you getting ready? We only have an hour before show time."

I jerk up. *An hour. OMG.* Suddenly the image of the President introducing me replaces my Dad. *What to wear?* I fly off the bed to my bags and start pulling out dresses, blouses, shoes, and a scarf. *Should I wear a scarf? This is bad.* I haven't even opened my bag, and now I have to get dressed, like immediately.

There are two dresses, two skirts, and three blouses; several are in my favorite color, green, and some in my close second, blue. A deep blue skirt that fits tight above my ankles is the winner, a green and blue patterned sleeveless blouse, and a fabulous loose fitting lace sweater-jacket that falls almost to my knees matches perfectly. One pair of heels fit, except my toes squish together. Standing, I take one step, my ankle twists and I go down flat on my face on the bed. How do tall, skinny models do this, I wonder. A pair of low heeled, embroidered slippers, with blue and green flowers on a gold background, are more my style. In front of the mirror, I do a slow spin.

My hair's straight as Angie's pontoons. I shake my head and stroke my hair a couple of times. It falls out and looks pretty good. OMG, that happens, like, once a year. As I admire myself, Samuel peeks into my thoughts. *I wish he could see me now, with real slippers.*

Three raps, "I'm ready," I call and skip to the door. Uncle Teddy stands adjusting his red, white, and blue tie. His eyes stare at the flats on my feet and scan up to my face. "Wow," his mouth hangs open. "You are …"

"Pretty?" I ask.

"Yes, more than pretty. You're gorgeous."

All I can do is laugh. He likes how I look, and I love it. For the first time I can remember, I feel really pretty. More than that, I feel like an adult.

"One more thing," he says, holding out a small, rectangular box. "I want to give you something to remember this trip."

I take the soft red velvet container and turn it in my hand. I crack the hinged lid and something inside sparkles against black silk. To keep from choking up I swallow, and open the box. Inside is a silver chain, with a pendant.

"After yesterday, I figured this was more than appropriate," he says.

Hanging from the chain, I watch a standing bear, paws raised and mouth open, reflect flashes of light as it spins. I can almost hear it roar.

I begin to blubber, "Thank you, thank you, thank you. This is so perfect. Really, this is one of the best days of my life already."

As I fit the chain around my neck, Uncle Teddy's door rattles with two sharp bangs. "Mr. Crenshaw. I'm here to escort you and Miss Carlisle to the conference room. Are you ready?"

"Show time," Uncle Teddy says, and kisses me on the forehead. "I'll meet you in the hall."

"Show time," I repeat, and take one more turn in front of the mirror.

Chapter Nineteen

The mood of the Black Scorpions darkens as Ark paces near the crevasse at the base of the wall. "We will follow our earlier plans. In exactly fifty minutes, we should have the distraction we need. Samuel, you and Fatuma are lost tourists. Change your clothes and descend the remainder of the hill." Ark's cadence increases as he walks faster. "Keep low and use the bushes and low trees as cover. When you hear the explosion, approach the shack from the east. They will be confused for only a minute, so move quickly."

Samuel tries to rid himself of his father's image, but the anger in Ark's voice holds him. Instead of his leader, he now sees Ark as a threat, someone who might harm him or anyone, at any moment.

"Be careful to stay out of sight until you reach the road." Ark continues, his voice rising. "Nakale and I will give you cover. Use whatever means needed to disarm the guards. After that, we will move to the back and secure the area."

Fatuma, eager to please, steps to the cave and pulls out shorts, shirts and other clothing. Samuel remains where he is.

"What is it my son?" Ark's voice softens, eyes relax. He puts his hand on Samuel's forearm. Samuel jerks back. "Are you all right?" Ark asks.

Samuel blinks to clear his head. Is he seeing Ark, or remembering his father? And who is he really afraid of? "It's nothing," Samuel replies as he refocuses on the moment.

"Nothing, of course," Ark says, pulling on Samuel's shoulder so their eyes meet. "You are my confidant, you know that? Without you, I can do nothing. If there is something wrong, please tell me now."

Samuel stares into Ark's deep dark eyes. The anger he saw, if at all, is now gone, only kindness and generosity remain.

"No," Samuel says. His confusion passes and he allows Ark to hug him. "I'm fine. I'll get ready now."

Ark smiles as Samuel walks to the cave. "Children," he whispers to himself. "They need constant firm guidance and absolute control."

Samuel removes his fatigues, pulls on three quarter length pants and a light t-shirt with an American flag and the word, Peace. He tries to keep his eyes diverted, and even feels his neck flush when Fatuma slips off her fatigues, steps into tight shorts, and boldly clasps on a bright purple, low cut, lace bra. Aware of Samuel's unease, she giggles and turns to face him as she pulls on a v-neck, crop top blouse. "Ready," she says, patting her belly. "Just another happy couple lost in Glacier Park."

Nettles grab and poke their legs as the two intruders slide down the steep hillside. "Stay with me," Samuel orders, as they crawl through brush to a small ledge east of the shack near the lodge.

"I see two agents at the shack, and one more agent at the back door of the lodge. That should be the kitchen."

Fatuma nods while she checks the clip on her pistol and holsters the gun in the small of her back. The first drops of sweat creep down Samuel's cheek. Although the air is warming, he recognizes the symptoms of nervous energy. Adjusting his pack, he hands Fatuma a red can similar to bear spray. "These canisters will shoot a tranquilizer pellet over thirty feet. Simply point and press the button."

She grunts, "This isn't my first rodeo, cowboy." The American expression surprises him and in an attempt to resist a laugh, he burps. Fatuma, equally nervous, catches the bug and begins to giggle. They both bury their faces in their packs to suppress fits of giggles and laughter. From above, it seems to Ark that one or both of his trusted assassins are sick to their stomachs.

"Shhh," Samuel manages to say, between gulps and hiccupped coughs. "We have … a … job to do."

Fatuma, who is curled in a ball, gyrating with hysterical giggles, squeezes her ribs in an effort to regain control. "I'm good—I'm good."

Samuel lifts his water bottle, points at Fatuma, and squeezes. "What the …," she says and swings at his arm. She catches herself moments before yelling. Her anger cuts like a knife through their silliness.

"What are you doing?"

"Just water," Samuel says. "Now let's get this done."

Samuel directs several squirts onto his face and underarms then passes it to Fatuma. "Make it look like we've been hiking," he says. "Your weapons?"

Fatuma pats the 9MM handgun in the small of her back and points to the outline of the AR15 rifle inside her backpack.

Armpits and the front of their shirts soaking wet, they slink down the base of the hill to the road, east of the guard station. Samuel checks his watch and looks to the front of the hotel.

On schedule, the earth vibrates as a plume of smoke rises near the far end of the parking lot. Attention is suddenly focused on the delegates in the hotel and the explosion in the parking lot. The Secret Service agent sitting in the front seat of an SUV moves to get out. The other agent raises his hand and says something.

Fatuma adjusts the top of her blouse, exposing her underwear. "Ready," she says. The two tourists, just out of sight of the agents, step forward at a lively pace. About fifty feet from the building, Fatuma waves and shouts in French, "Bonjour. Pouvez-vous nous aider? (Good morning. Can you help us?)" The agent, standing outside the right car door, glances from Fatuma to the explosion and back. Agents and body guards run like ants in all directions. The standing agent's walky-talky squawks questions and orders. They are warned to stop anyone entering the area, but the shock of the explosion and the surprise of the approaching hikers split his attention. He might have expected someone in combat gear, or possibly scuba gear, approaching from the lake. The last thing he expects is a French woman in shorts and open shirt hiking on the road. He reaches for the walky-talky, slides his hand to his gun, and takes one step forward.

"Halt, stay where you are. You are in a restricted area. Please state your business." The agent's hand rests on a holster strapped to his hip. He wears a flak jacket and an automatic weapon slung over his shoulder. His partner slides out of the car and stands behind the open door.

The innocent couple feign surprise and raise their hands. Fatuma says, "Non non. Nous sommes campeurs du Canada (No, no. We are campers from Canada)." In English she says, "Just camping. We have passports. What is happening?"

The agent's hand moves a fingers width away from his pistol grip. He senses something terribly wrong, but can't distinguish between his response to the explosion and the hikers. He doesn't want to over react.

Fatuma continues to speak in a soft tone, and pushes both her hands higher, as if to say, I have nothing to hide.

In times of extreme stress the mind sometimes plays tricks. In this case, the appearance of Fatuma's bright underwear freezes the agent's train of thought. He fixates on the bright purple. The second agent glances at him in question.

Samuel's left hand flips the canister up, aims at the neck, and presses the tab. Two almost indistinct poofs occur, and both men slump to the ground.

Samuel smiles, "Enough sedative to keep a six-hundred-pound bear down for twenty-four hours. They'll be out until tomorrow."

The dead weight of the two men is heavy, but the diversion works. Samuel at the head and Fatuma pulling the feet, manage to drag the agents to the side of the SUV. Ark and Nakale arrive in time to help lift the agents into the front and lean them back in the seats.

"There, there, little man," Fatuma says to the agent in the driver's seat as she kisses her fingers and touches his cheek. "You make everyone think you are on guard, while we do our business."

"Quick," Ark yells. "Secure their firearms. Our comrades inside the hotel have done well, but we have only minutes to get to the back door without being seen."

The opening speech at the environmental conference just concludes when the explosion happens. With the President at the podium, and the delegates seated at conference tables, agents and body guards take defensive positions. The bulldog agent stands by the President speaking into his handheld. "Yes—no—yes," he says. "Mr. President, we suggest an immediate evacuation of the conference."

"What was it, Hank?"

"A propane tank exploded. A cigarette seems to have been thrown into a dumpster. Foreign delegates and their guards smoke constantly, regardless of what we say."

"A fire?"

"Yes sir. It seems one might have ignited a fire near the propane tanks. We don't know if it was an accident or intentional. I'd rather not take a chance."

The President considers the recommendation. "Sorry Hank. This is too important and we're already here. Let's finish this today and leave late tonight." He nods toward the delegates who talk amidst a cloud of cigarette smoke. "Too many high-powered leaders to let them get away without addressing our primary environmental concerns, and introducing our guest of honor."

Hank nods as he scans the room. "As you wish Mr. President. I'll make the arrangements."

The four Black Scorpions skulk along the bank, close to the lake's edge. The rear of the hotel comes into view. Ark raises an index finger—only one agent stands guard. Fatuma adjusts her bra and stands. The agent's eyes widen as Fatuma raises her arms in surrender and her blouse spreads. His mouth opens as if to speak. Silent as a spider she slams both fists into his ears and down on his shoulders. The agent drops.

"I'll finish this," Ark says as his rifle butt swings toward the agent's skull.

"What are you doing?" Samuel whispers.

Ark's cold, hard eyes bore into Samuel, resurrecting the crazy father. "We do what we have to do." Ark kicks through the kitchen entry. The double-doors slam against the wall on the right and a stainless-steel table on the left, mixing bowls and trays of clam, crab leg, and sushi-style squid, fly across the floor. With a shriek the pastry chef tosses a large three-layer cake in the air, scattered chunks of lemon poppy seed cake and flags from twenty countries explode around the room. What follows is like a choreographed dance.

Chapter Twenty

In the lodge a five-foot log crackles and spits flames in an open pit fireplace at the end of the hotel lobby. Representatives from twenty countries talk amongst themselves and take one last glance out the windows before filtering back to their seats in front of the podium. Around the perimeter and between tables stand fifty-six black suits, eyes focused on their respective country's leader, prepared to protect them at any cost.

"My apologies for the interruption ladies and gentlemen," the President says. "It seems a cigarette, discarded in a trash bin near the propane tanks, caused a fire. The result was explosive. I know each of you are anxious to get back to work; however, I am assured we are under no further danger, so I suggest we continue and complete the conference today."

A few delegates clap and others nod.

"In any event, I've bent your ears about the purpose of our gathering and the financial implications of Global Warming for the past two hours. You'll be happy to hear I'm done for now."

A spontaneous round of applause erupts along with the President's laughter.

"Let us take a brief lunch break. Afterward we will meet Samantha Carlisle. Samantha is a courageous young woman who has a thing or two to teach us about how Global Warming affects us on the local level, and what can be done. We'll also have a chance for some of you to present local environmental issues and your solutions. With any luck, we'll move along without interruption and conclude our meeting by late afternoon."

Chairs scrape against the hardwood floor as delegates stand and reach out to the President, who steps through the crowd, shakes hands and slaps shoulders. Picking a slice of salmon from a deli tray, he excuses himself and, following his traditional conference schedule, walks to his room for a short rest. Two secret service men accompany him.

The square jawed agent with bulldog cheeks, Hank, speaks into a phone, "The Bear is on the move to the cave." He stands at the President's right shoulder.

"I need to freshen up, before we return." The President says. "Is Agent Henney escorting Ms. Carlisle and her uncle to the conference room?"

"Yes Mr. President." Hank checks his watch. "They will meet us in twenty-seven minutes. Mr. President, we've discovered a waiter who confesses he was the one who threw a burning cigarette into the dumpster and he is in custody. Although we are reasonably sure this was a careless accident, I'd like to take level orange action on your return."

The President nods, taking little notice. Threats to him and his family are constant. The Secret Service is always ordering some color-coded action or another. He seldom knows exactly what they mean, just another route or extra security. Prior to becoming POTUS (President of the United States), he thought colors were for crayons. Now they are security levels that disrupt his routine.

In his room, his personal attendant holds up a clean shirt. He slips his arms in the sleeves and takes the tie the attendant holds. "Don't make such a face," the President says, "people in the Northwest are proud of their salmon. It's a bit bright and not my style; but, I like the message. He holds up the silk tie with a jumping salmon and reads, "We Are All Connected."

The President looks up at the ceiling, reading his cell phone, as an attendant ties the gift. "There Mr. President, now everyone will see the word, 'connected.'"

Precisely twenty-six minutes later, the President, escorted by the two agents, walks down a long corridor. He passes the lobby elevator to the service elevator door marked, "Staff Only."

Hank speaks into his phone, "Bear is on the move, alternate route Zebra, podium in five."

The President stands to one side of the elevator as the doors roll open. Hanks steps in front while the other agent inspects inside.

"Clear," the agent says.

Hank steps aside and escorts the President to the far right corner. The lift clatters and shimmies on its descent.

"We will take an alternate route through the kitchen Mr. President. It will take a few minutes longer."

"No problem Hank. It will give me a chance to thank the staff."

The elevator bounces once and stops with a thud. The doors creep to the side to reveal the bright room clad in stainless steel. Hank fills the exit and surveys the setting—a head chef behind one end of a stainless steel table; an assistant at the other end of the table, and a pastry chef at a second table. The three chefs glance up, startled for a moment. "As you were," the head chef says and wipes her hands on her apron.

"Clear," Hank says and steps to one side.

"Good afternoon," the President says. His enthusiastic voice echoes off the walls as he sprints to the head chef to shake hands.

"I hate this glad-handing," Hank mumbles to the junior agent as he directs him toward the stairs and tries to keep pace with POTUS.

The President steps forward and bends over the long table holding an elegant arrangement of Dungeness crab, oysters, shrimp, and a three-foot salmon filet. "Looks like we're having the world's best seafood today," he says and extends his hand toward the assistant chef at the other end of the table.

"Yes sir," she says, reaches out with her right hand and clasps the President's palm. A flash of light catches Hank's attention—a twelve-inch carving knife in the assistant's left hand. Hank reaches for her arm. The junior secret service agent turns toward the President. At the same moment, the double entry doors slam open, mixing bowls and trays of clam, crab leg, and sushi style squid crash across the floor. With a shriek the pastry chef tosses a large three-layer cake in the air, decorated with twenty country flags. What follows is like a choreographed dance.

The President hears the crashing of bowls as cake bits and tiny flags fly through the air. Out of the corner of his eye he sees a tall, slim, man in black push through the double doors. Three people, firing weapons, follow.

Pop! A sound echoes off the walls like a champagne cork, Hank's junior agent gasps and falls. Hank's fingers touch a pistol inside his jacket as the assistant chef pulls the President's hand, leans forward, and slides the edge of the carving knife against the President's neck. "Don't move," she says in a flat, steel cold voice.

Hank freezes. The head chef turns—another pop comes from the direction of the kitchen doors, she falls. A scream forms in the mouth of the pastry chef—pop, he goes down. Hank's hand clutches his pistol—pop, and the bull dog's legs buckle. He slumps to the floor.

Fatuma checks her gun. Her cheeks wrinkle in a smile, "I'm out of tranquilizers. My next shot is a bullet."

The President remains bent over the seafood platter with the razor-sharp blade pressed to his neck. The assistant chef looks at Ark and nods. "Look who I have," she says. The President raises his hands to shoulder height, "Enough. What do you want?"

"Shut up," the assistant chef yells.

Ark grabs the President's left arm, and twists it behind his back. In a single motion, he pulls the President's arms together and binds them with a plastic zip tie. The President's jaw clinches swallowing a groan. "There's no need ...," the President begins.

"Quiet," Ark says, and slaps the back of the President's head. Ark kicks the back of his legs and pushes on his shoulders; the President collapses to his knees. "Not one more word or you go down for good. Understand?"

The President nods in silence.

Upstairs, Secret Service Agent Henney approaches the staff elevator. A waiter carrying a large round tray loaded with dishes holds the sliding doors open and bows to let her board first.

"Thank you," Agent Henney says as she enters. "Smells like something good for lunch. Too bad we don't get to join in." The waiter smiles in agreement. Under his rolled-up sleeve she notices a tattoo of a black scorpion. "Nice tat," she comments.

The waiter steps in behind her. As the doors clank shut, he tips the tray far to one side. Agent Henney reaches out, "I've got it."

Her hand touches the edge of the tray as the waiter's free hand slips inside his jacket, grips a pistol, and fires one shot into her side. The stun-gun makes a muffled bang. Agent Henney's eyes widen, her lips begin a word, and she slumps to the wall and falls. Over her phone, he hears, "Bear is on the move …"

The elevator door slides open. The agent on the second floor turns to inspect IDs—there is a pop. The agent reaches out and the waiter pulls his arm. He falls over Agent Henney's legs. In the elevator, the waiter pulls the Lock button, removes the agent's jacket and slips it on. Checking the hall, he straightens his back and marches toward Uncle Teddy's room.

Chapter Twenty-one

Aknock rattles my hallway door. I finger my new necklace, make one more spin in front of the mirror, and swing the door open. Uncle Teddy and an escort stand outside. Something strikes me as wrong. Uncle Teddy's energy is frozen and sharp. The agent wears black pants, a white shirt, and a jacket that somehow doesn't fit, although I can't identify why not. The scent of stale food surrounds him.

I think to ask Uncle Teddy if he's okay when the agent steps to one side. There is a gun stuck in Uncle Teddy's ribs. "Do exactly as I say and you will be safe," the man says.

I stutter or cough or something, and he says, "Do as I say. We're taking the service elevator, no stops. If either of you try to talk or move away from me, the other will be dead. Understand?"

Uncle Teddy's eyes form slits under pulled together brows. He gives a short nod as if to reassure me or say, do as he says. "You walk in front," the waiter orders me. He keeps his hand on Uncle Teddy's shoulder and, in lock-step, walks behind. The clicking of my shoes on the hall floor reaches me like in a dream, and my mind does a cart wheel spin.

The lift doors are open. Instinctively I jerk back; our captor pushes me and I step on something soft. A woman agent lies on the floor under a serving tray. Falling sideways I step on the hall guard who lies partly over her, a stain on his pants. The smell of urine surrounds me.

We don't speak. To my side Uncle Teddy's profile transforms, eyes red with anger, nostrils snarled and pulsing. He appears like a wolf, frozen in the moment, ready to attack. I keep expecting him to smile and the President to step in, laughing and telling me it's a joke, but there is no President and, no matter how much I hope, I know it isn't a joke.

The doors scrape and slam shut. "Push B," the imposter agent says and pokes my back. Like a robotic tool, my arm reaches out. I shake so bad my finger misses the button twice before connecting. The floor bounces and we descend.

"Flip that switch to Express," he says.

I stare at the lighted numbers as they flash two, L, then B, without stopping. The doors open. A rush of air sweeps in flushing our brief prison, and his fingers push against my back. I stumble forward with Uncle Teddy behind. In one take, I see the President on his knees with a tall man in black standing over him.

"Oh my gosh," I scream, hands to my face. Samuel stands near one wall. I lunge forward wanting to cry out to him, tell him about my new slippers, warn him about the imposter agent with the gun. A hand grips my shoulder. I spin around and my back and head smash against the rough kitchen wall. His arm against Uncle Teddy's neck, and his other hand against my chest, the imposter agent says, "Do not move, or everyone dies."

We freeze, my heart pounding, my breath short—my only thought, to warn Samuel.

Chapter Twenty-Two

Pressed against the wall, I take in a scene resembling a food fight—a really bad food fight. To my left a woman in shorts and a small man, really a boy, in fatigues stand in front of the double doors leading outside. They each have some kind of machine gun. At the back wall a female chef lies on the floor covered with cake. Closer, another chef lies on the floor. At the table the President crouches on his knees. A woman chef holds a knife to his neck. The tall man in black stands over him with a rifle slung over his shoulder. Samuel stands to my left against a wall. He sees me and slides to a crouch. He looks alone, abandon.

The tall man's chest heaves. One side of his lips form into a half smile, "This is very accommodating of you," he says to the President. "I did not expect you to welcome me. I thought I would have to hunt you down." He looks at the agent imposter who guards us. "Have you called?"

The waiter squeezes my arm as he responds, "Now?"

"Yes, now, you idiot. Call them. Tell them he is delayed—talking to the staff or something."

The man's hand releases. He kicks the bull dog agent, and when he doesn't move, grabs the agent's phone.

"This is Bear Watch One." He listens for a moment. "Yes, POTUS is in the kitchen talking with staff as usual. We'll be an extra fifteen."

As he speaks, I think about yelling for help, but my lips are rubber and I can't form the sound.

"Tell the diversion detail to delay fifteen. I'll call as soon as POTUS is on the move," the man says, and nods as if someone on the other end of the phone is in the room. I swallow and he pushes his fist into my collar bone. I choke and bile stings my throat.

The tall man grunts, and pulls the President to standing by his suit jacket.

"I believe you already know who I am," the President says, his voice as cool as ice. "To whom do I owe the pleasure?"

"You are an arrogant jackass, but since I now own you, I'll answer. I am Arkimedes Manuel Litvinov, the man who controls your life."

"Mr. Litvinov, and what is the purpose of this dramatic meeting?"

Amongst the chaos, the President's smooth tone surrounds us like a cool lime smoothie, creating order out of insanity.

Archimedes lets out a long sarcastic laugh that cracks through the cool and brings crazy to the front again. "You think formalities will improve your situation?"

"I believe that even under the most difficult conditions, we can remain gentlemen," The President says.

Archimedes' brow rises. He glances toward Samuel, "Very well, let us be gentleman. You owe me this pleasure because my, our, mission is to destroy the bane of humanity, the cause of all suffering in our world, the cruelest socially corrupt theory ever conceived by man—Capitalism."

"Ah, I see," the President says as he shifts his hands and winces. "You somehow feel that if you capture me or others at this conference, you will end this *bane of humanity*?"

"Yes," Archimedes says with a sweep of his arm. "We will cut off the head of the dragon and render it helpless."

The President's eyes move to me and Uncle Teddy. "I see. But why have you taken these workers? They are neither the head of the dragon or the tail. They simply provide services. Why not let them go and we'll discuss your demands."

At this, Samuel rises up and steps forward. I try to speak, to warn him, but the man's fist chokes my words. Stop, they're bad people, I want to say.

"He's right, Ark, we don't need these people," Samuel says. "They mean nothing to us. They are extra baggage."

What? Why is he speaking to that man? Why is he calling him Ark? Wait, wait …

"They can be locked in the store room," Samuel says. "There are six of us now. We can complete our mission and be gone."

Ark's face twists in what appears to be a spiral, like clay on a potter's wheel. His eyes flash blue from inside dark sockets as he examines the room. A window that looks out on the lake catches his attention. "The airplane?" One crooked index finger points to Uncle Teddy. "Are you the pilot?"

The following silence angers him and he pulls out a pistol, pushes it against the President's temple. "Are you the pilot of that plane? Answer me, or I'll end this now."

"I am," Uncle Teddy says. I'd seen Uncle Teddy this way in the elevator. From the side, his face narrows and he crouches, again the wolf ready to lunge. I blink and he returns to normal, except his eyes remain bright red.

Ark steps toward Uncle Teddy swinging the pistol like a wand. "So you fly the float plane?" he says, waggling the muzzle under his nose. Uncle Teddy jerks, and the fake agent pushes him so hard his head bounces off the wall. Uncle Teddy's lips purse. He spits. The wad lands on Ark's cheek. A moment later, Ark slams his pistol into Uncle Teddy's jaw and blood splatters across my face. A warm pungent smell fills me. I urp and swallow stinging bile. Uncle Teddy's knees buckle. I reach to catch him and Ark's arm rises again, to swing on me.

"Wait! There is no need to harm a child," The President says. "Tell me what you want and we'll work this out."

Ark turns a pirouette, his gun perched over his head. "No need?" he says with vinegar in his voice. "What do you know of need? You are one of the privileged. Everything you stand for supports your way of life."

I flinch as Ark's wrist sweeps close to my nose.

"But what of these servants you call workers? What do they gain from your accumulation of wealth?" Ark leaps to the woman in shorts. She smiles as if enjoying the attention. "Here is Fatuma, a woman who, only a few years ago, was held in slavery. How does she benefit?" The smaller boy with the machine gun across his chest steps back as Ark rushes to him, arms spread like a game show host. "And, what of Nakale? He was a boy soldier held captive and forced to guard diamond mines or be killed. His captors mined jewels that are sold to the rich, finding their way to necklaces and rings that your wife now wears. Capitalism," he yells so loud the dishes shake, "Capitalism is the cause of the world's suffering, and we will end it now. The head … the head of the dragon will be cut off today." His voice rises to a crescendo as he advances on the President, face to face Arks cheeks taught, lips trembling, "I will end it with your life."

Samuel steps forward, "We're not here to kill anyone."

"Shut up," Ark shrieks.

We? My Samuel said we. It doesn't make sense; he's talking like one of them. My mind cramps and again I feel stinging spit in my throat.

"My life means nothing," The President says, his face equally taught.

"You'll say anything to save your own life," Ark yells.

What happens next is the last thing I expect. Blood pulses in my temples. My hands shake and my knees tremble. The stink of blood stings my nostrils. I want to help Uncle Teddy, who pulls his legs under him and crouches on the floor with his blood-stained shirt against his face. Instead, I hear myself speak, like another voice coming out of me, steady and strong. "He's right, killing the President won't change a thing."

The fake agent pushes harder to stop my words. Ark swings around. His pistol barrel pressed against my forehead like a branding iron. Cold shivers creep down my spine. "What do you know, servant girl? What knowledge do you have about the world?"

The cold metal of the gun barrel shocks me into the realization that my big mouth challenged a maniac—a maniac who could kill me at any moment. I sneak a peek at Samuel; his face tight, brow creased, eyes filled with questions. I take a breath, "I don't know much, but I took a civics class and learned about our government."

Oh my gosh, c'mon stupid, you can do better than this.

Ark throws his head back and a long cackle creeps out, "You took a civics class?" This seems to humor him. He lowers the pistol and makes a deep bow. "Forgive me, you are an expert. And what did you learn in your civics class?"

"I learned the President's right," I pause. "No one person runs the government. I mean, Capitalism is about free markets and all that, not our government. He doesn't really have anything to do with our financial system."

Okay Sammy, you can't stop now.

"We have three separate parts," I take a deep breath, praying I can remember, "Legislative, Judicial and the President ... the Executive. But he's only one branch and even there he has to jump through all kinds of hoops to get anything done. Anyone watching can see that it's mostly politics, just arguing and fighting. Hardly anything gets done."

The President, who has remained totally chill, lets out a low chuckle. "She's right. We spend most of our time defining words rather than taking action."

"Shut up," the fake chef with the knife says.

Ark moves so close to me his stinko breath warms my cheek. "So you think the President is just a puppet with no responsibility?"

"No," I stammer, "well, yes, I guess so."

Think Sammy, think.

"What I mean is that killing the President is almost like killing me." *I can't believe what I just said.* "I mean our government isn't run by one person." My voice steps up an octave and words fly out like from a machine gun. "If the

President's gone, the Vice President steps in, and if the Vice President's gone, the ..."

"Speaker of the House," The President says.

"Yes, Speaker of the House, steps in, and if he's gone someone else steps in, and it continues until no one is left, and that's millions of people. We don't have one head of the dragon, we have millions, and you can't kill all of us."

The words shoot out before I realize what I'm saying. *Had I just invited him to kill us all?*

"You're all the same," Ark says, "brain washed into believing your system is the best."

"No," Samuel calls out.

I turn. The back of Ark's hand and his huge wristwatch fly at me.

Everything goes black.

Chapter Twenty-Three

My head throbs. A flat cold surface lies under me, and something damp puddles around my cheek. I try to lift my head. Pain, like from an ice pick, shoots through my neck. My vision blurs and light flashes. I realize the liquid and the sweet odor is my own blood. My stomach convulses and I throw up.

"Don't move," Uncle Teddy's voice drifts down to me like ashes from a fire. "Stay down Sammy."

I relax my arm and hug the floor as my stomach continues to spasm. My head jerks as Samuel bends down and sets a damp cloth on my forehead. "Here, press this against the wound. It will stop the bleeding."

Until he hands me the napkin, I don't realize what causes my pain. Now it makes sense—Ark hit me. I press the damp cloth to my face, and my fingers touch a doughnut around my right eye. It's totally shut.

"What's the matter with you," I hear Samuel yell. "There is no reason to harm these people. And a child? That won't serve our end."

"Don't question me," Ark shouts, "I'm in charge here. I run this unit. This is my operation."

"Unit? Operation? We're not an army. This isn't an operation," Samuel says as he stomps toward Ark. "In your words, we are a movement, protestors against a financial system that leaves billions of people in poverty while the rich get richer. You said we were here to call attention to the evils of Capitalism, that extreme action was necessary to wake up the world. Anger, you claimed, was the best motivation for action, and with news organizations in each country reporting on this conference, it was our chance to ignite that anger and mobilize the poor behind us. Now, instead of a protest to gain awareness and understanding, you beat up a child and it sounds like you want to kill the President of the United States."

Ark's face flashes red and his eyes spasm right to left. "It's too late, Samuel," he screeches. "We have come too far. I did not want this any more than you, but you heard him. The President will not listen, and neither will the leaders upstairs. Ark's arms wave wildly as he steps over the head chef. To move our cause forward, we have to create chaos, and chaos is best created by a disaster. We have the G20 in one room. We have the President of the United States on his knees as our hostage. We have moved beyond getting attention. Now is the time for dramatic action. We must cut off the head of the dragon."

"Cutting off the head of the dragon is just a metaphor," Samuel yells. "It is not to be taken literally. And dramatic action? We hardly know what we're doing. We carry guns and threaten people. We've already set off one bomb as a diversion. Now we're holding the most powerful leaders in the world and you threaten to kill them. We aren't protestors any longer, we've become terrorists."

Anger, the best motivation for action.

I shift and blink to better see what is happening.

What is Samuel talking about? I know anger. I've been angry since my mom died. I hate my dad most of the time, but to kill? That's not anger, that's crazy.

I raise my head. Samuel stands toe to toe in front of Ark. They're talking, arguing like two children.

Could he have lied to me? No, he's a protestor, like he said. He wouldn't kill. I've looked into his eyes—he couldn't kill.

"Shut up," Ark orders. "Fatuma, do you have the package?"

"Of course," the woman in shorts says, nudging her backpack with her boot.

"Open it and arm the device."

"The device?" Samuel says. His face clouded with confusion. "We used the device already."

Fatuma sets her rifle against the wall and kneels. She removes a large square box covered in bubble wrap, and strokes the box as if it were a pet cat. She smiles at Ark. "It's here, at your service."

Samuel glances at me and Uncle Teddy. He closes his eyes. When he opens them, the pupils have expanded to cover his beautiful brown iris, hard and determined.

"The entire area is on alert by now," he says and moves closer to Ark. "The President's delay will certainly trigger a total lock down, if it hasn't already." He grips Ark's arm and leans in, as if confiding in him. "You are right. Now is the time for action. We will do what we need to do, but we will need everyone to get out of here alive."

"Everyone?" Ark repeats. His lips move, counting, sizing up the room. "Yes," he kicks Uncle Teddy's leg, "this one can fly the plane and the President guarantees us safe passage out of here. But her?" Ark points his gun at me. I duck as our eyes meet. Ark puckers his lips and cocks his head to one side. "Wait, I know you," he says.

My breath catches. I freeze.

"I've seen you. In the news?" He glances out the window. "San Juan Express. How stupid of me. You are the sea lion girl. Only months ago, you captured poachers in the San Juan Islands. They were ignorant fisherman. None the less, the papers played it up as a great feat. And now this ugly pig," he points his nose toward the President, "wants to use you to promote his Capitalist agenda. You are the girl everyone talked about." He lowers the gun and smacks his lips as if he had finished a meal. With a spin, he swings his gun in a circle. Everyone in the room ducks. "We have a celebrity amongst us ladies and gentleman. You are right Samuel; we can use them all." He raises his hand and directs the barrel at my head. In reflex, I turtle my head down. "Although, she may be more valuable dead. It would send a clear message."

"I won't fly the plane without her," Uncle Teddy says. "You kill her, you'll have to kill me, and you'll never get out of here."

Ark shifts the gun to Uncle Teddy. He taps his nose with his crooked finger. "You will be on your best behavior with her life to protect, so yes, we will all go. Such loyalty, it is what makes you American's so endearingly weak. You'd rather save one, than save the world."

I feel Uncle Teddy's breath near my ear. "Maybe we'll do both," he whispers.

Chapter Twenty-Four

The imposter agent speaks frantically into a phone. "No, no, they will kill POTUS if you do anything to stop them. They are ready to die for their cause. Just assemble the delegates and their guards in the lobby." He presses his palm against the ear piece. His face scrunches like a prune. "No, you're not listening to me. You can't follow protocol now. POTUS is a prisoner with a gun to his head. They—will—kill—everyone."

The man's face twists in frustration. "No, I don't know how many ..."

Ark grabs the phone and pushes it to the President's ear. "Tell your servants to obey or else."

The President speaks methodically, "This is your President." His eyes close for a moment, "I want you to do exactly as they say. Focus on protecting the people in the hotel. Follow the chain of ..."

"Shut up," Ark yells and pulls the phone to his ear. His face shakes and his nose and cheeks flush scarlet. "Listen to your puppet President, you dog. Clear the grounds around the float plane and guarantee us safe passage, or I kill him and all of you. Do you understand?" Ark's eyebrows pull together and he nods in approval. I flash an image of a bright red Grinch. The phone hits the tile floor and cracks open. He smashes it with his heel.

"Solomon, are you and Patrice ready?" Ark says. The assistant chef steps to him and bows her head. The imposter agent bows and Ark puts his hands behind their necks, as if in prayer. They stand silent for a minute and he whispers, "You have fulfilled your obligation. Our plans have changed and I cannot take you." The assistant chef's head shakes and she wipes her eyes. "I want you to go upstairs. As soon as the elevator doors open, you will be taken. You are free to act as you will. You are my heroes." The two look at each other in silent communication and walk to the elevator. Unarmed they step in and, like a prison gate, the wobbly doors shut.

Ark glances down to Fatuma, "Are we ready?" he asks.

"In a moment," she says.

"Let's move."

His pistol pointed at the President's neck, Ark grabs him by the shoulder. "We're going to walk out of here to the plane. If anyone gets cute, we're all dead, understand?" No one responds. "Understand?" he yells. There must have been an acknowledgement, because he pushes the President toward the double doors. "Get ready," Ark says.

To my amazement, Samuel grabs Uncle Teddy and wraps a strap around his neck like a dog collar. He jerks, and Uncle Teddy coughs loud. His swollen lip hangs over his chin, and blood drips across his shirt as he tries to stand. Fingers pinch my shoulder. I look up at the boy, Nakale. Through my one good eye the world appears like a telescopic image, round and fuzzy, and the kitchen spins like a carousel. Nakale jerks and my cheek separates from the floor with a popping sound.

Sometimes your brain feeds you information you can't believe you're receiving. Uncle Teddy slips his keys out of his pocket and slides them under the freezer. I'm sure they'll catch him, but Samuel focuses on making him stand, and everyone else looks toward the kitchen door, except Fatuma. She crouches over the small bubble wrapped box with wires stringing out each side. I blink to clear my vision. *A bomb*, my brain says. *Holy crap*. I struggle to move away, but Fatuma makes a sharp angular swing at my knee and lightning explodes through my leg.

"Stay where you are," she orders.

On what appears to be an old flip phone, she pushes a few buttons. "There," her lips crinkle in a sardonic grin. "Now you will go out with a bang."

"She goes with me." Uncle Teddy chokes out through the neck strap.

"She goes," Ark agrees. "Nakale, bring her."

Fatuma grunts her disapproval. Nakale grabs the back of my neck and I let out a shriek. He jerks me up. I stumble forward and the boy's machine gun slaps against my side. Behind Uncle Teddy, my body slams through the double doors into blinding sunlight.

Chapter Twenty-Five

After the smothering kitchen, I'm dizzy in the mountain air. Nakale, shorter than me, is strong enough to force me forward. We leave a trail of blood from the kitchen to the plane.

"Hurry up," Ark says, and pushes the President into Angie, slamming the President's forehead into the door frame. Fatuma climbs into the back seat beside the President and pulls down her blouse to reveal a totally slutty purple lace top. Tears drip down my cheeks as Samuel jerks the dog collar to force Uncle Teddy around Angie and into the pilot's seat. The information feeding my brain is more than I can understand. *Please tell me this isn't happening*, I pray. *This is my Uncle Teddy and the President of the United States.*

I blink, hoping I'll wake up as Samuel scrambles into the back seat. The President shifts sideways and Fatuma lands an elbow to his chest. The President slumps forward, his hands bound behind him. Ark pushes past me into the front seat next to Uncle Teddy, who looks at me and nods, as if to say we're okay. I try to smile, and everything stops. I realize Nakale and I are the only two left standing outside the plane. I make a jerking movement toward the only remaining space in Angie, but Nakale pulls me back.

"Only room for one," he says. "Looks like you stay after all."

A bony hand pushes past me to Nakale's shoulder, throwing him back. "Hurry, you inside," Ark says pointing at me. "Nakale, you in back."

Nakale glances from me to Ark. "No room in back. Maybe ..."

"No," Ark yells. "You climb in the storage compartment, or you stay."

Fatuma's long fingers, wrap around a blanket, and push it forward, followed by her hysterical laughter. "Here Nakale, this should keep you warm."

The next moment Nakale pushes my head into the door frame, turns, and runs down the trail along the lake. Ark raises his weapon, but lowers it immediately. "Let your agents kill him," he says to the President.

Ark's voice jerks my attention to him. "Get in."

I slide onto the seat and wince as my butt lands half on Arks leg. He wraps his arm around me. "Good," he says, "Nice and cozy." He lifts his gun toward me and looks at Uncle Teddy. "You have sixty seconds to get us out of here."

Ark's arm tightens around my waist and I have the sudden urge to pee on his leg. Beyond Ark's beak nose Uncle Teddy, the wolf, sits frozen, eyes on the control panel.

"Move," Ark says.

A gust of wind shakes Angie as Uncle Teddy pats his jacket pockets. "My keys. I don't have them."

"What! Is this a trick?" Ark's hand pushes on my back, and my head slams forward. "I'll shoot her here if you play with me."

"No, no," Uncle Teddy pleads. My keys must have fallen out in the kitchen. I'll get them. Please. I can find them."

The two men lock eyes. Uncle Teddy must have planned this as a possible way of escape, but I tried not to think it. I was terrified Ark might sense his plan. Uncle Teddy turns as if to leave.

"Wait," Ark says. "Samuel, take the girl and find those keys." Ark's elbow presses into my ribs and I fall from the plane. With a pistol to my head, my Samuel half carries and half throws me toward the building. Above, along a row of windows, men in black suits with rifles track our movement.

The kitchen is like entering a war zone. Blood covers the doors, counters, and floor. Food spreads across everything. Bodies point in all directions, and in the center sits a ticking bomb. He pushes me forward, and I'm happy when, instead of searching for the keys, he crouches near the box. "We've got to disarm this thing," he says.

He's part of a terrorist gang, but I knew he wasn't one of them. He's a protestor—kind of.

"You don't know anything about bombs, do you?" he asks.

Something snaps in me and I laugh. *This is serious,* I tell myself, but the laughter keeps coming. I kneel beside him and notice a digital counter on the phone—00:37. My laughter stops. *Only thirty-seven—thirty-six—thirty-five seconds left.*

"Are you kidding?" I yell. "I don't know anything about bombs. You're the terrorist—er, protestor. You're supposed to know about this kind of thing. It's your bomb."

"It's not my bomb," he insists, raising his hands. "I didn't know they were bringing this thing. I'd never agree to kill people. I just wanted attention. To tell the world about Capital …"

"I know, your stupid Capitalism movement. Oh my god, are you an imbecile? Ark is fricking crazy and you still think this is some kind of noble movement? OMG."

I don't know anything about bombs, but even I can tell this is a countdown to a really bad ending.

Red, blue, black, yellow, and green wires run from the phone to the box.

"Cut a wire," I say, for no other reason than seeing people do that in movies. Samuel's fidgeting fingers move back and forth over the wires, but don't stop.

"Do something," I scream. "We have to do something."

He stares up at me with soft puddled eyes. Tears drip from the corners as he turns his head side to side. "What wire?"

He's not moving. He's going to let us die.

I push his shoulder and grip the red wire.

The timer reads 00:09.

Eyes shut tight, I pull. I'm not sure what I expect, a loud bang, a pop, or maybe absolute nothingness. The wire springs loose, it's not even connected and nothing happens. Not dead yet, and neither is the counter. Samuel bends forward pushing himself over part of the box.

He's trying to protect me.

"Get off you idiot," I say.

My fingers slide over the yellow wire, then the blue wire. The timer reads 00:05. They don't feel right. Something attracts my hand to the green wire, my favorite color. The timer clicks 00:02.

I grip the thin wormlike strand. With all my strength, I jerk. My body falls forward over Samuel. The box leaps off the floor as the wire holds. I yank it again and squeeze my eyes tighter. Images of Uncle Teddy in his leather flight jacket, Loren and his clown outfits, Liz and her sunshine smile, and my mom and dad, pass like a slide show as I wait for the end. A sweet smell rises up. Samuel's hair, his sweat surrounds me. The muscles in his back flex and I hug him.

I hug him for four, five, six-seconds, which, I realize, means we aren't dead. Or, at least if we are, we're dead together.

Oh my gosh.

I sit up, to be captured by Samuel's saucer eyes. We both look down at the counter—00.00.

"Why didn't you do something," I demand.

His eyes search the room. "I couldn't move," he says and blinks several times. "But you, even in slippers, are amazing."

We sit on the kitchen floor, me and my protestor/terrorist, and he calls me amazing. I raise my hands and shrug. "Just lucky I guess."

He looks down at the bomb. "Yes, you're very lucky, and I'm not very good at this."

"No. You're a lousy terrorist."

He lets out a short nervous laugh. "Lousy," he agrees. "Even so, now we need those keys."

"Don't worry," I say and scramble to the freezer. "I think I know where to find them."

I relax talking with Samuel, but as my knees and palms stick to the bloody floor, I'm reminded I am a prisoner.

"There is another problem," Samuel says, as I stand holding the keys, "Ark."

My expression telegraphs my disgust.

"I don't expect you to trust me," he says, "and I don't like this any more than you. I never intended this. I truly came to make a point about the injustice of the Capitalist system, not kill anyone."

"He's crazy," I say, and turn toward the elevator door.

"I can't," he says. "If I let you go, Ark will kill me and your Uncle and probably the President.

Every part of me wants to run, but he's right. If angered, the maniac will do anything, and I can't risk their lives. "What about the bomb?" I ask.

"I'll tell him it was a dud or the timer broke, and I'll make sure you get your chance," he holds his hand out for the keys, "but for now we return to the plane. You'll sit next to the door, so be ready. Taking off or landing will be your chance to run. As long as Ark thinks you escaped on your own, he won't hurt anyone."

Samuel reaches for a backpack left on the floor and pulls out a pair of fatigue pants and light weight boots. "Here, put these on and grab that coat hanging on the wall."

I hesitate, then turn away to pull on the pants and slip off my skirt.

Something gnaws at me—*Why didn't he even try? Did he fall over the bomb to protect me or stop me?*

As I pull on the boots, he holds the jacket up and I push my arms into the silky down.

"Listen Sammy," he says, "I had no idea Ark was this crazy. I'll figure a way out of this and protect your Uncle and the President—I promise."

For that moment, he is the gorgeous Frenchman in a red beret, helping me. The next instant, he pushes a gun in my back.

"Run," he says.

Chapter Twenty-Six

Angie's engine groans, coughs, and catches. Black smoke curls up the sides as Uncle Teddy spins a wheel on the dashboard to adjust the flaps. He increases the throttle. A high wind pushes waves up on the lake as Angie slides onto the water and slaps across the wind chop. High mountain ridges rise up each side as we speed toward the end of the lake. Slower than expected, we lift off and shoot down the valley. It's afternoon and the sun's reflection on the windshield blinds me.

"Hang on," Uncle Teddy pushes the throttle to full, and pulls back on the steering yoke. "We're overloaded and aren't getting enough elevation. C'mon," he coaxes Angie, "just a few more feet."

Tree tops and branches whip past the windows. Uncle Teddy pushes forward on the yoke and at the last moment jerks back. Angie lurches down, then up, and seems to stop in mid-air. The engine noise dies.

"Hold on," Uncle Teddy yells as the tip of a tree slaps the left wing and Angie spins to one side. We lose speed and direction, but the lift from our upward momentum elevates us inches above the mountain ridge. Like an eagle, Angie sails out over a sheer cliff and St. Mary's Lake fifteen hundred feet below. My stomach lifts as Angie sputters, and her nose dips. She gains speed.

"We're descending too fast," Uncle Teddy says as he pulls back on the yoke. "You can do it Angie, pull us out of this."

There is a collective gasp and I squirm on Ark's bony knee. He tightens his arm around my waist and points his gun at Uncle Teddy. "What is happening?"

Uncle Teddy scans the control panel, and clicks a few switches. "We're almost out of fuel. The engine's not responding. I'm not sure."

"You don't carry fuel?" Ark demands.

"A fuel truck was scheduled to arrive tomorrow. We never got refueled."

Ark pushes my ribs with his elbow and twists toward Uncle Teddy. "Where can we land?"

I can put down on St. Mary Lake, or with some luck, maybe Two Medicine."

"Out of the park," Ark orders.

"The only way out is east, over the Blackfoot Reservation," Uncle Teddy says.

We descend fast. At times, Angie gasps, chokes, and swoops dangerously close to the water. At others, she roars and we gain altitude.

"The low fuel level must have allowed contaminants into the fuel lines. I'll nurse her along as far as I can."

"Get us out of the park," Ark yells, turning the gun on me. "And head for the reservation."

The ten-mile-long lake is a narrow strip of freezing glacial runoff. Uncle Teddy keeps Angie near the center, and prepares for an emergency landing if her engine stops. I turn to watch the conversation and notice Samuel, his dark eyes fixed on me. I glance at him and he nods once to the right. Through a mist of confusion, I remember his words, "Taking off or landing will be your chance to run."

What? You're kidding. Is he telling me to jump?

Ark's gun still points at me, but he looks at Uncle Teddy. I peek at Samuel one more time. His eyebrows narrow and he gestures to the side again. I'm not sure exactly how, but as Angie lurches closer to the water, I push the door and roll. The roar of Angie's engine changes to a raging chorus of engine noise, propeller spin, and wind. My butt leaves Ark's leg, and my back thumps off a pontoon. I am a rock in free fall. Reflections flash off the water. Angie's tail lifts over me as my cheeks rattle and my legs churn in a running motion.

I realize what I've done at the moment I hit water. There is no splash, no bounce, just a thunderous explosion and bubbles. I go straight down for miles. The concussion knocks the wind out of me. I instinctively gasp, and suck in water. My lungs contract, I cough and inhale more liquid. I flail and grasp for the surface. My mouth, nose, sinuses, and lungs fill with water. My head balloons to the size of the moon. I kick one last time, and let out one more cough. Everything sinks into a deep spiral, darkens and, like the closing of a lens, goes black.

Chapter Twenty-Seven

A pin point of light appears. I blink. It expands, and explodes around me. Something pushes against my ribcage, and I hear myself scream as I fight for breath. Through coughs and gasps, I jet toward the shore like a speed boat with no engine. I swallow water, bounce over rocks, skid on mud and roll. A musky, dank odor surrounds me, and a soft muzzle nudges me up the bank. Water gushes between my teeth and out my nose. Oxygen comes in short gasps, yet I am calmed by a presence. I reach out to catch myself, and my fingers find a mushy ball with two holes. I grip it like a bowling ball. It snorts and gives me one last push. Yellow grass settles under my back. The tender eyes and long snout of a moose peer down at me. I hack. She snorts again. *I'm okay, I think.* As I stretch up, she stomps both front hooves, turns, and lopes down the lake shore. The humongous rump of the moose meanders away until I can't see her, yet I sense something.

Nearer, in the tall grass and damp brush, there is another pair of eyes. The eyes blink and flash a speck of gold. Pushing my hair back, I sit up and shake my head. Water sloshes in my ears, or brain. The brush rustles, a cowboy hat rises above the grass and the Indian boy appears. Breeze whips the trees above me as he steps forward. In the background, the last of Angie's engine roar disappears over the horizon. My heart skips. My mind's eye sees the plane falling from the sky and I imagine what will happen to Uncle Teddy and the President—and Samuel.

My panic must show, because Runs with Fire smiles, "They're okay," he says. His soft hand rests on my shoulder. "Come Nitakein," he beckons, "we will find them."

Runs with Fire takes my hand and time seems to stop. My body, bruised and beaten, suddenly feels healed. The terrible ache in my head disappears, and without trying, I stand. He moves and I follow, without effort. I can't say exactly, but we walk, run, and even fly—I think. Like a fairytale, we sweep through pastures that stretch out of the park, and over a low ridge of mountains that define the western edge of the Blackfoot Reservation. We communicate without words as he talks about his people.

"Because you are special," he begins, "you perceive me in all forms, and hear my thoughts."

His gentle communication tickles and I find myself laughing often.

"Many of my own people only know me as human. They have forgotten our heritage and our connection to all things. In sweat lodge ceremonies, we reconnect with ourselves and our spirit. But to become the spirit, that is rare. That is not the fault of the people. It is what happens when a people are forced to separate from their tradition."

We move rapidly away from St. Mary Lake leaving the green forested Rocky Mountains for the beginning of the Great Plains that extend east to the Mississippi River.

"Our land," he continues, "was always without borders. The white man's government created lines that divide our people. We have many names, including Niitsitapiiksi, real people—speakers of the Real Language, and Amskapi Pikuni. Niitawahsi is the name of our territory," he raises his hand and sweeps it north, "which originally extended from the Northern Saskatchewan River, south along the eastern slopes of the Rocky Mountains to the Yellowstone River."

"Canada? Did they live in Canada too?" I ask.

"There was no Canada or United States. We saw no borders, just open land where our people roamed and prospered. We believe this land was given to us by Creator, the source of all life. We roamed freely, hunting game and collecting plants. We moved camp frequently, always with a purpose, never depleting resources. We were one with nature, and still are. Over many centuries we welcomed other tribes to trade, but never to hunt our game. We protected our domain, as did they."

We fly over hills of golden grain and fields of yellow sweep beneath my feet. Heat waves dance before me, carrying the warm sweet smell of wheat. As Runs with Fire speaks, I have a vision of the Saskatchewan River flowing four hundred miles north, and the Yellowstone River, three hundred miles south. I imagine herds of buffalo roaming the prairie and painted warriors on horseback stalking them. There are villages, thousands of people living in teepees, children playing and hundreds of horses.

A small lake sails below. We rise over a knoll, and the earth turns dark. My imagination becomes reality; a herd of bushy brown bison appear. The temperature drops and the sweetness turns to heavy dust. Just as quickly, we sweep left, away from the herd, and touch earth. I run as hard as I can, Runs with Fire's arm around my waist, until we slow and slump on the ground.

"Our people lived in harmony with the land for centuries, until the Napikwiin, White Man, came," he says. "They brought disease, bullets, and whisky. What smallpox and measles did not kill, whisky and wars did. Our people, the Niitsitapi, original people, fought early mountain men, but in the mid eighteen hundreds settlers came on what is now the Oregon Trail, and the great iron horse soon followed." He turns to face west. "In Glacier Park they show pictures of early tourists arriving on trains, but what is not shown is the death and destruction that came before them."

Runs with Fire's face contorts as he speaks. His eyes water and his hands shake when he talks about the death of his ancestors. Similar stories, in books and movies, were entertaining, but I'd never connected the stories with real people. Now I sit with a Native American, an Original American, and his pain moves through me. I can't speak.

"With the railroads came hunters who shot the Linii, buffalo, for sport. Thousands lay dead or dying as the iron machine snaked its way through our windswept grasslands. We are told that between 1870 and 1890, tens of thousands of buffalo were murdered. Less than one thousand remained."

I scan the horizon. Dust rises from what appears to be a single animal covering the earth. "There must be thousands in this herd," I say.

He rises up on all fours, his back arches and stretches. "Yes, there are thousands now. Bison are a protected species, unlike Native Americans." His eyes sparkle gold. "This is not a complaint, it is history. Today we treat our land, as always, with respect. We are grateful the American government has protected each lake, trail, mountain and valley in the park."

I want to ask more, but Runs with Fire is already on his feet. He brushes his pants and points toward a single tree that stands on a knoll beyond the herd. "Your people, Nitakein, are there."

Cold surrounds me and I'm surprised by my sense of isolation. Until that moment, I'd felt one with Runs with Fire, but I suddenly become aware of a great gap between us. No matter how much I reach out, his world is oceans, eons, away from mine. I want to protest, to say they aren't my people. I want to hug him and tell him he is my people, to help him, to save him.

Hearing my thoughts, he smiles and drops his gaze to his boots. "Thank you, Nitakein," he says, "but that is not possible. We do not need to be saved. We need equality and respect—from outsiders and ourselves. Slowly, that is happening. And yes, you are my people too."

"My name is Sammy. Why do you keep calling me Nitakein?"

He smiles. "Our word for sister," he says as he walks in the opposite direction of the tree. His voice is silent, but I hear him. "From the tree, follow the smoke. There, you will find your people. It is up to you to save them. Know that I will be close by and, above all, trust yourself."

With his words, his back lengthens and he begins to jog. Within a blink, he is gone. I stand alone. The President and Uncle Teddy are somewhere over the hills, and I am their only hope.

Great. I feel like an overused punching bag, and I'm supposed to save the leader of the free world.

Chapter Twenty-Eight

"Grab her," Ark yells as Sammy rolls from the plane. He grabs her jacket and the smooth material slips off her arms. Ark holds only an empty coat. Confused and angry, he fires one shot through the jacket. The side window shatters. He lets out a manic shriek, "She'll never survive the fall, good riddance."

Ark spins on the President and yells at Teddy, "Get us out of the park."

Uncle Teddy's first reaction is to turn and search for Sammy. He feels her hit the pontoon, and he drops a wing to assist her fall.

"Keep flying," Ark orders. "You do as I say or, I swear, we'll all die now."

Teddy's face twists; his brows narrow to a single line.

"She's dead," Ark yells. "Now fly."

Torn between searching for Sammy and Ark's order, Uncle Teddy feels a chill, like the blood draining from his body, a sensation he experienced when going into combat as a young fighter pilot. He squeezes the steering yoke until his knuckles are white. "You keep threatening to kill us, so go ahead," he says. "Pull the trigger if that's what you want. I don't give a damn."

Ark twists to the President. "If that's what you want, I can accommodate you."

With great reluctance, Uncle Teddy levels the wings. He flips the auxiliary tank switch and jostles the throttle in unison to Angie's coughs to maintain flight.

"Do your best Ted," The President says, "God willing, Samantha will survive. For now, just take us as far as you can."

Ark holds the gun on the President. He faces Samuel who trembles with anger. "You are upset," Ark says. "I understand. You liked the girl."

Samuel hesitates, "I—didn't like her, but I am sorry to see her die."

"It is better," Ark says, "She is a hero, remember."

Samuel shifts and looks out the window. "Now she will be a hero forever."

Teddy dips one wing and whispers a silent prayer that Sammy's special sensitivity, and every animal in the forest, will take care of her.

Angie passes over the east end of the lake, and descends quickly. A golden rise of wheat and grass comes dangerously close. Uncle Teddy jockeys Angie up and down to maintain as much altitude and speed as possible. St. Mary Lake disappears behind them as Angie swoops over a knoll, and the open plains of Montana spread out like a shimmering yellow table cloth. Far to the right is a cluster of buildings, a small ranch. Ahead, a blue button in the gold appears.

The cabin noise is tremendous, and exhaust bellows in through the broken window. "There's a lake about a half mile ahead. I'll try to make it." Teddy says.

Ark leans forward, and points, "What is that?"

The President laughs, "They're buffalo, American bison."

"Not the animals, you idiot, the buildings."

"It's a ranch," Teddy responds.

"Yes, yes, I see the farm. Is that equipment next to the barn, tractors, a car, and some other vehicles? Motors need fuel. Can you run on gasoline?"

Teddy doesn't respond.

Ark smiles. "Thank you. Your silence is my answer. Take us down there."

"This is a float plane," Teddy protests. "I can land on water or a runway, but a pasture."

"Land at the farm," Ark repeats. "Just do it."

Angie makes a bumpy turn to the left, and Teddy lines up on an open field near the barn. The engine sputters and Angie drops enough that Fatuma, who had not moved a muscle since take off, jumps and covers her mouth with her hand. Everyone's arms rise as their butts lift off the seats. Teddy pulls up, jiggers the throttle—then silence.

"Hang on," he says.

With the last sputter, the only sound left is the rush of wind passing the fuselage. The engine's last gasp leaves a black plume of exhaust that smells of oil. Angie sails for seconds, and begins to drop. Brown dirt and yellow grass speed past so fast Teddy doesn't notice the drainage ditch until the last moment. Angie's pontoons hit first. The right strut hits the ditch and collapses. She spins a one eighty and tips forward on her propeller.

Inside, the occupants bounce like ping-pong balls in a tumbler. Fatuma, who has neglected her seatbelt, pitches forward. Hands bound behind his back, the President jerks sideways and lurches forward pushing Fatuma into the instrument panel. She screams as sharp screw caps dig deeply into her face and eyes. Both Fatuma and the President slump into Ark who extends his forearm for support and smashes into the dash panel. If asked, Fatuma might remember the breaking sound, as his arm collapses backward.

Samuel and Teddy, the only two who remain conscious, both wear seat belts and are tossed violently. Samuel's head slams into the ceiling, and blood spurts from a small cut. Teddy bangs into the upper windshield and sits slumped over the steering yoke.

"Are you all right?" Samuel asks.

Teddy hesitates, unsure who Samuel is talking to, he shifts and pain explodes in his side. "A few broken ribs maybe," Teddy says with contempt. "Otherwise I'm fine."

"You're bleeding from your forehead," Samuel says.

"Back at you."

The two men inspect each other. Both have cuts across their face and hands. Blood oozes from multiple wounds and swelling twists and bloats their features. Fatuma moans and shifts her hand.

Samuel raises his chin toward the door. "Get out of here."

Teddy's head tips. Has he heard correctly? Samuel waves his hand and whispers, "Get out, run."

Teddy's flight training taught him to think fast and analyze situations in an instant, but the order takes a moment to sink in. This may be his only chance. Can he leave the President? It is unlikely Ark will kill the President as long as he can be used as a hostage. As for Teddy, Angie is down and Ark will not hesitate to get rid of him since he is no longer needed to fly the plane.

Angie rests like a tripod, one strut in the ditch, one wing pushed in the ground, and the broken propeller buried in the dirt. Teddy's door is on the high side. He pushes and his ribs scream with pain. Black smoke rolls out of the engine and a small flame sparks to life. Using his arm, Teddy props the door open and slips through the opening, leans forward, and free falls eight feet onto grass and rocks. The landing is a full flop on his back. Dizzied by the pain, he takes a minute to survey his options. The house and barn are closest—Ark will search there first. An old car sits nearby and beyond is a small shack. He shakes his head, blinks several times, and crawls and limps toward the out building.

Over Ark's motionless back, Samuel watches his captive escape. *I shouldn't be here*, he thinks. Under his palm, Ark shifts and Samuel's thoughts shift to his leader. *I'm sorry, I've let him go.* The shack door closes and Samuel is torn by his many choices. *I've made a terrible mistake.*

Flames lick up around the propeller. Samuel reclines as Fatuma coughs and pushes against the dash throwing the President into the backseat. His limp body falls on Samuel who pretends to be unconscious. Fatuma's eyes water with pain, perspiration, and blood. She instinctively reaches for the pistol on her waist. A sharp pain explodes from a bruise the size of a basketball in the small of her back. Touching the gun grip, she considers what she has wanted to do since they arrived—shoot the President. Ark will kill her if she does, yet she smiles at the thought. She wipes her face, blood smears across her fingers and cheek. In front, Ark slumps forward. He does not move. Her anger and hatred for the man next to her surges, but her love for Ark dominates her response.

"Archimedes," she whispers.

Ark does not move.

She reaches out and touches his shoulder, "Ark."

He remains motionless. Her fingers instinctively grab his shoulder and in panic, she yells, "Ark."

His body jerks upright, he bangs his head against the ceiling and swings his elbow hitting Fatuma on the cheek. He grabs for her throat.

"Ark, it's me," she says, gripping his hands.

Ark's rage matches Fatuma's. He tries to throw several punches before he realizes his arm hangs helpless, and recognizes Fatuma. She ducks to avoid the worst of Ark's attack, and when he stops to look at her through swollen eyes, for a moment she imagines he might hug her.

"The dog?" he yells.

"He's here, still breathing." Fatuma says, elbowing the President's shoulder. Her nudge produces a groan. Samuel remains quiet throughout the fracas. Only when the President moves does Samuel pretend to come to and feign confusion.

"What the …," he mumbles, and pushes the President upright. "What happened?"

Ark and Fatuma begin to talk over each other, Ark throwing accusations and Fatuma deflecting them with apologies. The President regains consciousness, but remains silent. Samuel surveys the situation. He knows Ted is gone. Most likely Nakale and Sammy are dead. Now he must choose—the President—or Ark.

"The pilot," Ark roars as he struggles to regain control. His eyes drawn immediately to Samuel, he searches for an answer. Samuel's face is blank. Ark refocuses on the sun faded old car. "Forget the pilot," he says. "We'll take the car. Everyone out, now. Bring your weapons."

Fatuma utters obscenities as she wiggles free. Ark fills the cabin with profanity until he rolls out the door, over a pontoon, to the ground. Samuel follows him. Fatuma wraps her arms around the President and pulls him to the high side door. Head first, hands still bound, she pushes the President out of the plane. At the last moment, Samuel grabs him around the chest and lowers him to the dirt.

"We need him. It does us no good if he can't walk," Samuel says.

Fatuma grunts and spits in their direction.

"Hurry to the car," Ark says and pushes the President, who falls to his knees. "To the car," Ark repeats, and presses his gun to the President's back. Ark searches for Teddy as they cross the yard, knowing he is nearby, but confident he has no weapons. Together, like survivors of an old west shootout, the four stumble, hop, and drag their way to the banged up old Ford parked by the shed.

"Throw him in the trunk," Ark says and pushes the President toward Samuel. Ark holds his broken arm, raises one foot to the side door, and kicks.

Chapter Twenty-Nine

An eagle soars over, casting a sweeping shadow. A mushrooming dust cloud forms as the herd of bison approach. I crouch on one knee behind the tree, and extend my neck. About a mile away, a small black spiral of smoke appears. Around me are small bushes and clumps of sage brush. I pause and hear clearly, "Follow the smoke."

My movement takes on a whole new dimension. I rise to walk and my feet seem to lift off the ground; I run and distance disappears. In moments, I see Angie, tipped at an odd angle, doors open and smoke rising. Ark, Fatuma, the President, and Samuel hobble toward a faded blue, dust covered car. My eyes dart across the scene, and my heart stops—Uncle Teddy isn't with them.

Ark kicks in the driver's window, while Fatuma jerks on the passenger door.

"Damn car," Fatuma yells.

"I'll blow this thing to pieces," Arks says as he pulls out his pistol.

Samuel holds the President's arm and steps him toward the car's trunk. While Ark and Fatuma focus on getting in the car, Samuel turns a handle and opens the trunk. There is a moment of indecision before he makes a break. In a breath, all hell breaks loose. Samuel pulls the President's arm, dragging him toward the house. Ark, at first confused, hesitates, then fires three shots. Fatuma shouts something and shoots twice. The President stumbles onto the porch, red spreading from his thigh. Samuel opens the door and pushes him into the house.

My Samuel is trying to save the President.

Instead of following, Samuel turns to face Ark. He takes one step forward. There are explosions and Samuel falls back toward the door. Two red circles form on his shirt. A scream forms as I push my hands against my mouth. I stand and Fatuma wheels around. Her arm extends and one eye stares down the sights of her pistol pointed at me. The eagle squawks and a wisp of wind touches my cheek; I whisper, "No."

The barrel of Fatuma's gun is like a cannon, ready to blow my head off. I sense Runs with Fire and my shoulder twists. She fires a shot. Like a humming bird, the bullet whistles past my ear. The next moment, dirt and dust swirl in the air. Horns, fur, and hoofs thunder past as hundreds of buffalo swarm the yard. I shade my eyes; a cloud of animal and earth thunder around me. Dust particles stick to my eyes and fill my nose. I taste chalky dirt. Stumbling back, my forearm presses across my eyes.

Like a summer storm, the stampede ends as quickly as it came. I wiggle my toes and fingers. They are still connected. Dented and smashed, the car pushes into the ground—a metal cow pie. Fatuma lay off to one side twisted in an unnatural shape. I search for Ark and shiver; he's gone.

The most important person to me is also missing. I want to yell out, to call for Uncle Teddy, but I know I have to be silent. Instead, the Indian boy's advice comes to me, and I close my eyes.

Help me. Please help me, whoever you are.

I open my eyes; my knees buckle and a deep freeze washes through me. Ark stands twenty feet away.

This was not the answer I hoped for.

His clothes are torn and bloody grime covers his body. One arm hangs at his side, the other holds a gun.

"You are the biggest pain in the arse," he says. I'm not sure if he is complimenting me or insulting me. "You need to die. Maybe this will take care of you."

At first, all I see is the muzzle of his pistol, another huge cannon. Then a brown object lumbers behind him. I close my eyes tight and open them—it's still there. My heart leaps as I recognize the stench of the grizzly bear, the one I'd met on the trail the day before. Don't stare, I tell myself. I don't want Ark to notice, but I can't help it. The bear is as big as the old car.

Like when I was running, time takes on a new dimension. Everything seems to slip into super slow-mo. Ark's words come out garbled. His movements, like a slo-mo movie, flicker frame by frame. When the bullet leaves the barrel, it sparks and flashes. Spinning, it buzzes like a bumble bee as it flies so close I feel the heat on my neck.

The next instant I'm back to normal speed with the grizzly behind Ark. She rises up, twice his height and lets out a roar. Ark turns and fires a shot. The bear doesn't flinch. He fires the pistol again; this time it just clicks. Click, click, the pistol cries in desperation, until with one swipe of her giant paw, she catches him by the shoulder. Ark lifts, flips, and lands on his back. With the grizzly lumbering after him, he scampers backward, an upside-down crab. The grizzly takes three steps and places her paws on either side of his head. She roars again. Slobber and goo drip onto Ark's forehead and down his cheeks, into his—yuck—mouth.

Uncle Teddy, where are you?

In a dead run, I head for the cabin and push through the slightly open door. Dust puffs from under my feet as I stomp in. I sneeze three times. My eye adjusts to the darkness. The President is on his back near a pot belly stove. Samuel is on his side near a wall. My toe catches and my knees skid near the President's head.

"Mr. President." Bending forward, "Mr. President."

He raises his head and looks into my eyes. "Samantha," his eyes widen and he smiles, "you're alive."

I pat my cheek, "Yeah, I think so."

"Am I happy to see you."

"We're okay, Mr. President," I assure him. "The buffalo took care of Fatuma and Ark is outside, guarded by a bear. You're safe."

"Buffalo? A bear? Did you hit your head?"

"Yeah, but I don't know where my Uncle Teddy is. I have to find him."

He struggles to sit up, blood soaked dirt covers his face and body. He has a large cut on his forehead and there is blood on his leg. "I don't quite understand the animal references," he says, "but if you can remove these bindings. I'll help you search for Ted." He twists to expose his slip-tied wrists.

A knife from the counter cuts through the plastic bindings. He leans on my shoulder and we shuffle to the porch. Blinded by sun, I shade my good eye and choke back tears. Uncle Teddy drags himself across the dirt yard. I leap forward, and leave the President to stumble and catch himself on a post. I've never been so happy and relieved. One step and I fall to the ground. Tears stream down both our faces. You don't know how much you love someone until you think they're gone, and at that moment we both seem to have that realization. We hug for a few minutes, tears and snot covering our dusty faces.

"Sammy, Sammy," he keeps saying. "You made it. I can't believe you survived."

"I'm here," is all I can say.

"I think you need to postpone your reunion," the President says. He stands near Fatuma, holds her pistol and points it at the grizzly. "I'm beginning to understand about the bear reference. But, we might have a problem."

I giggle at the most inappropriate times, but the look on the President's and Uncle Teddy's faces is totally hilarious.

"It's all right," I say.

Standing, I pull Uncle Teddy up, and cautiously walk toward the bear. She turns to face us. Her butt presses on Ark's entire upper body. She makes a low grunting sound and, if I'm not mistaken, farts. Choking back laughter, I notice the President still holds the gun.

"Mr. President, you probably shouldn't point that at her. She's really trying to help."

He clears his throat and lowers the pistol. The gargantuan animal sways side to side. Ark's legs kick like a helpless wind-up toy.

Everything's okay, I think. *Thank you so much for your help. I'll take it from here.*

The grizzly turns her massive head to me. Instinctively, I slide back an inch. She sways back and forth, lets out one more growl that shakes the earth, rises up and poops on Ark's face. She steps off. Ark lay frozen, super glued to the ground, and covered in bear crap.

The bear shuffles toward me, rises up and faces the President. It takes me a moment, but I realize ... "Mr.

President, I'd like you to meet—that is, ah, let me introduce you to—the Presidential Bear of Glacier National Park."

The President slides the gun into a back pocket. "Pleased to meet you Presidential Bear," he says. He does not extend his hand. She seems to like the introduction because she tilts her head and gives a muffled growl. We stand for a minute, not knowing what to do next, when she roars, and throws spit and drool on the three of us. She falls to all fours and turns. It is delicious—not the spit, but Ark, covered in crap, flat on his back, cursing, while the provider of stinky gifts sways her huge butt across the open field.

I giggle, until I remember Samuel inside the cabin. In the commotion, I'd forgotten him. My nervous laughter again turns to chokes and sobs.

"Samuel," I say, and run. He's on his side, blood pooling around him. What can I do? He isn't moving or, as near as I can tell, breathing. I sit for a moment until the President kneels beside me. His hands on my arms, he holds me.

"It's alright Samantha. It's over."

No, I don't want it to be over, not like this. Nothing is all right.

Chapter Thirty

Lines in Samuel's cheeks deepen, and his color pales like ash. I stroke the curls stuck to his neck. "Samuel," I whisper. "Please wake up."

"He's gone," The President says, and squeezes my shoulders.

"No," I plead. "He can't just die like this. He didn't mean it. He tried to help."

"Nitakein, you're okay," a voice comes from above.

Beside me stands a pair of gray and black cowboy boots, jeans, and a t-shirt with a picture of four Indians and the words, "The First Homeland Defense." His black hair hangs in a long braid from under his dusty old cowboy hat. It is Runs with Fire, who looks like any other boy of the prairie. I scrunch my eyes and try to find traces of the spirit boy who brought me here, but he is all human. The President, startled, tries to stand and step between us.

"It's okay Mr. President," I say, and motion for him to stay seated. "This is my friend, Runs with Fire. He lives here."

"You are not injured. That is good," Runs with Fire says. "But this man, he looks bad."

"I'm afraid he's mortally wounded." The President says.

Runs with Fire steps around us and bends over Samuel. "May I?" He places his hand on Samuel's forehead and his other hand on his heart, closes his eyes and is silent. When Runs with Fire looks at me, the gold diamonds are there, yet his face is weary. "I must leave you now, but I will return. I hope all is well with your friend."

I begin to protest but, as he has so many times, Runs with Fire vanishes.

"He's awake," the President says.

My hand jerks on Samuel's neck, and he coughs. Blood comes from between his lips and he rolls to one side. I scream and pull him onto my knee as he convulses and spits up red-black liquid.

The President touches Samuel's neck and shakes his head. "He seems to be recovering. I don't know how, but he's back."

Moments later Uncle Teddy slams the door open and stumbles in. "Ark's taken care of. I wired him to a post for safe keeping. He's got bear scat all over him, just like the scumbag deserves."

Light falls on Samuel's cheeks as he struggles to rise. "Stay down," I say, holding his shoulder. "You've been shot. Like I told you, you're a terrible terrorist." He apparently doesn't like my joke because he throws up in my lap.

"We might get some water from this old spout," the President says, pushing to stand. Through the doorway he spots the empty yard and looks at Uncle Teddy. "Did you bind Fatuma as well?"

Uncle Teddy's silence is our answer.

In the yard, Angie sits tipped forward. A single tiny flame spurts from a tube, like a first birthday candle. Under the fuselage, legs edge toward the front of the plane. A moment later, Fatuma breaks into a run toward Ark, with a machine gun in hand.

"I see her now," Uncle Teddy says and dives for the floor.

A spray of bullets burst through the cabin, shattering the old wooden siding. I reach forward and help Samuel crawl across the floor to cover. I lean over him.

The President retrieves the pistol and turns it over, as if to study it.

Uncle Teddy holds out his palm. "Maybe I should do that Sir."

"Yes, I think that might be a wise choice," the President says, and passes the gun over as wood chips fly around us.

Uncle Teddy slides on his side to the doorway. He holds the pistol at arm's length, and takes careful aim. Fatuma yells profanities and rages with the rifle, yet Uncle Teddy stays calm, waiting for the right moment.

As the fire fight rages, I cover my head and feel Samuel push me aside. He holds a pistol in the air, pointed at the President. "I'm sorry Sammy," he says. "I choose Ark."

Choose Ark? What does that mean? Choose right, choose life. No, you can choose anything but Ark.

A wail vibrates through my chest as my heart shatters with the realization that Samuel is following Ark's command to cut off the head of the dragon. I bring my hands down hard on his body and push his arm. A single bullet lodges in the ceiling. Still screaming, I slam my fists repeatedly on his arms and chest.

"How could you?" I scream. "You lied to me. You are a murderer."

He fires a second shot and there is a pain, like a branding iron on my skin. The President does a knee drop on Samuel's wrist and twists the weapon away. With shaking hands, he points the gun at Samuel's forehead. "Don't even breathe," he says.

Beyond the chaos of Fatuma's automatic weapon and Samuel's attempt to kill the President, there is a rhythmic pulsing. First it is an echo, then a thunderous chorus of turning blades. As quick as I hear the first whup—whup, choppers lower from the sky and soldiers, in full battle dress, jump from the open doors of the helicopters. In seconds, they spread out in the farmyard, rifles trained on Fatuma and Ark. Fatuma pauses, but holds her ground. A single female soldier approaches. With the coolest calm, she sneaks up behind Fatuma, and in one motion wraps her arm around Fatuma's neck and slams her to the earth. I don't think the soldier is aiming, but Fatuma lands in a pile of bear poop.

Three paratroopers approach the cabin with caution. They pause at the doorway and step in, rifles pointed in every direction. The lead trooper yells, "Clear."

The bulldog, Hank, steps through the doorway. He bends to pick up the pistol Uncle Teddy dropped, and retrieves the pistol from the President.

"Mr. President, we've secured the grounds and we need to get you out of here, now." Seeing the President's injuries, he asks, "Are you all right sir."

"I'll be fine Hank, thank you. This man is a terrorist and needs to be arrested, and Miss Carlisle and Mr. Crenshaw both need medical attention."

Hank speaks into his walkie-talkie. "We're clear, POTUS is safe. Get paramedics in here immediately."

Samuel is next to me on the floor, his shackled arms twisted behind him. Two soldiers lift him. He tries to speak but I look away and they hustle him out of the house. Uncle Teddy sits with his arm around me. A medic applies bandages to the President's face and leg. Covered in dirt and blood we form a circle of disaster. My chest heaves, and I lose it.

Chapter Thirty-One

We stay like that, all of us bandaged like mummies. I'm sandwiched between Uncle Teddy and the President, blubbering, coughing and spreading tears all over them—until a soft voice calls my name. As if from nowhere, Runs with Fire stands in the doorway. Startled and surprised at his sudden appearance, Hank reaches for his neck, ready to drop him where he stands.

"It's okay Hank," the President says. "This is a young man from the reservation, Samantha's friend."

Hank hesitates, and with great reluctance releases him. Hank does not move away.

Runs with Fire steps forward and kneels next to me. "Nitakein, you are injured."

Until he said that, I hadn't realized I was bleeding. Samuel's shot must have grazed me.

"May I?" Runs with Fire asks. When I nod, he reaches his palm over the five-inch-long gash in my side and closes his eyes. A fiery pain increases then disappears. He smiles, stands and extends his hand. "Welcome to the Blackfoot Nation, Mr. President."

The President grips Hank's hand and pulls up to stand. He hesitates, brushes his palms together and squeezes Runs with Fire's hand.

"Thank you." The President says. "I'm sorry about all this mess. We made quite an introduction to the Blackfoot Nation."

A dead silence surrounds us as the President inspects both his palms and continues, "Are you from here?"

"Yes," Runs with Fire says, "I live in the next valley with my mother, aunt and uncle, and cousins."

The President's eyes scan the horizon. "This is beautiful country. You must love it here."

"Yes, it is beautiful. But, we love all our land, including that which is now Glacier National Park."

The President catches the reference and, although I hear the President is never lost for words, he is then. He stammers and asks, "Do you farm this land?"

Yes, my father was a farmer and now the land is managed by my mother and brothers.

The President nods and clears his throat. "And your father?"

"He passed. He drank whisky until there was nothing left of his mind and body. It happens on the reservation."

The President nods, "Yes, it happens. I'm sorry."

"How sorry, Mr. President?"

The President jerks upright. His shoulders square, as if he's being attacked. Runs with Fire does not balk.

"You can help Mr. President. Many of us do well, like my uncle who is an artist and has a gallery. My family manages our farm. We have wheat fields and raise horses. Others do not do as well and have many things they need: good schools, treatment for addictions and a homeland that is better than the dry dusty reservations many were forced to one hundred fifty years ago. And when natural resources are discovered on our land, they should not be taken from us. It is time we receive what was promised."

Stunned by the machine gun list presented by the articulate and knowledgeable young man in a dusty cowboy hat, the President stands motionless.

"Yes, that is something I can look into," The President says. His words are flat and carry barely enough energy to leave his lips. Without responding, Runs with Fire turns and steps away. His boots clunk across the wood floor with a solid defiance. As he steps off the porch he leaves the words, "Action, Mr. President, not words," ringing in the air.

A silence as broad as the Great Plains surrounds us. Hank inspects the floor as if to find and pick up the disrespectful comments. I'm stunned. I've never heard a boy speak to adults, let alone the President, that way. A wave of shame washes through me for the treatment of Runs with Fire and his people, and a sense of pride rises in my spine for the skinny Native American boy who speaks his truth. I watch as he transforms into a trail of dust and his words, "Nitakein-Sammy, you are my people," sing in my head.

The President is silent for a minute. "It makes you think," he says. "We take for granted what we are given, or have taken, and seldom think about the other side of that coin."

He focuses on the vast prairie beyond the bullet ridden cabin wall. "I wonder if there can be a time when, instead of winners and losers, there can just be winners?"

He shakes his head, and with Hank as a crutch, steps out onto the dirt grounds and moves toward Ark.

"Mr. President, please," Hank says.

The President stops. Fatuma and Ark, bound in handcuffs and straightjackets are held by soldiers. Fatuma spits and spittle dribbles down her chin. They both jerk and are led toward a chopper where Samuel, bent forward, sits turned away from me. A row of paratroopers create a human hallway for the President to reach a larger bird near the shed.

Paramedics patch cuts and bruises on me and Uncle Teddy. From our seated positions on the porch, we wave to the President while a commando jogs toward me. "The

President wants you and your uncle to go with him," he yells through the chopper noise. He takes my arm and I half run, and am half carried, to the chopper.

"Welcome aboard," the President says with his usual cheerful smile under a large bandage across his forehead. He leans to my ear, "This has been quite a day. We're going back to the conference and I'm going to finish that speech. I can't miss the opportunity to lecture twenty world leaders." He stares directly at me, and for the first time, I notice he has big chocolate eyes too. "If you are up for it, Samantha, I'd still like to introduce you."

Uncle Teddy starts to say something, and an inner voice speaks to me, *Speak Your Truth.* I lean forward. "Yes Mr. President. I'd love to be introduced at the conference."

"You're a heck of a kid, Samantha. A heck of a woman," the President says and lets out a long laugh. Uncle Teddy begins to laugh too. Soon a nervous, relieved, heartbroken laughter fills the cockpit, to be drowned out by whup—whup—whup. I touch my stomach, completely healed at that point, as we lift toward a clear blue Montana sky.

Chapter Thirty-Two

"Ladies and gentlemen," the President begins. "I can't tell you how happy it makes me to speak with you this afternoon."

Chairs scrape against the aging wood floor; attendees stand as one. For several minutes, palms slap together in an ovation for the President. Excitement swirls through the crowd while several leaders whoop, holler, and wave their arms in the air. Uncle Teddy and I sit off to one side at a round table with two Secret Service agents. We try to stand, but Uncle Teddy winces in pain, and I'm only able to lean forward. Commandos in flak jackets have replaced the waiters and service people. I nod toward one soldier with a machine gun slung over his back, and a pot in one hand pouring a cup of coffee. I point to Uncle Teddy's empty cup.

Uncle Teddy leans toward me, "Thanks, I need something to keep me up." He nods toward the podium. "I don't know how he does it. He just keeps going. Against all advice, he insisted on one more hour to finish his presentation. As soon as he's done, they'll get him out of here and clear the building. It will be closed for the season."

Earlier I'd gone to my room to shower and change, and would have loved to wear my jeans and t-shirt. Instead I settled for a frilly dress I don't particularly like, and those wicked heels. My feet kill me. Now, the President's speech quiets the crowd.

"My fellow leaders, you are all aware of what happened today, my abduction, the attempt on my life, and on your lives. What you do not know is how it ended. Fortunately, for us, the young lady I am about to introduce was a part of the resolution. Originally I invited her here to highlight Global Warming and our responsibility as leaders to take action to protect our environment, our species, and the world.

You don't need me to lecture you on the particulars of climate change, and how, as a result of an increase in what is called the Greenhouse Effect, the earth is warming. Most scientists agree that by our contributing to an increase in specific gasses that block heat from escaping from our atmosphere, we are increasing the Greenhouse Effect and accelerating Global Warming. Decades ago we identified the destruction of our Ozone Layer as a threat to humanity's survival. In the Montreal Protocol of 1987, one hundred ninety-seven nation states came together to reduce the use of chlorofluorocarbons and today the hole in the Ozone

Layer is shrinking. Therefore, we know, with collective action, we can have a dramatic and positive impact on our environment.

Politicians still argue the cause, but we must all now agree the earth's atmospheric temperature is rising. Regardless of the cause, this warming is changing our lives in many ways, from melting polar caps and rising sea levels, to rising temperatures of both aquatic and oxygenated environments. Entire islands and nations are threatened and disappearing. This has changed living conditions, and killed animal and plant species. Food production is diminished, resulting in famine that affects vast swaths of people.

Science tells us that action on a global scale is needed to turn Global Warming around and avoid catastrophe in your countries and mine. The terrorist attack waged against us at this convention punctuates how fragile our hold on life is. I was reminded today, by a wise young man, that actions are more important than words, and action is required—now."

He promised to keep his speech short and to the point, and I jerk to attention when he begins my introduction.

"To emphasize this point, it pleases me to introduce Miss Samantha Carlisle. Samantha is a young woman who, three months ago, risked her own life to identify rogue fishermen who were killing seals and sea lions in the Pacific Northwest of the United States. When no one believed her, she forged ahead, determined to protect the animals she loves. She was kidnapped, and after masterminding her own escape, facilitated the capture of the rogue fishermen."

I feel eyes on me and warmth rises in my neck as I squirm in my chair.

"Today, she again demonstrated her courage during the terrorist attack we all experienced. Her wisdom, courage, and persistence in the face of doubt and skepticism are an apt metaphor for this gathering. Ladies and Gentlemen, join me to welcome Miss Samantha Carlisle. Samantha, please come up and join me."

The President waves his hand and still wearing my silly salmon necktie, he flashes his bright smile. I stand. My knees buckle. A giggle swims through the room. I push, and this time I rise up by holding the back of Uncle Teddy's chair. Three steps and my right heel twists. As I go down, ready for a face plant, a Secret Service agent catches my arm. Straight as a toy soldier out of the Nutcracker, he escorts me to the podium. While I approach, a few people stand and clap, then more. By the time I reach the President everyone is clapping, just like they had for him.

"Well, Samantha," he says, "we've had a long day, so if you don't want to, no problem, but, is there anything you would like to say?"

The applause dies down, and I look around at the one hundred or so people, all smiling for me. My mouth opens and words begin.

"Thank you. I don't have a speech prepared, so I'll just talk about my experience. I come from the San Juan Islands off the coast of Washington State. Just like people here, in Glacier National Park, and at your homes, I believe I live in the most beautiful place in the world. Wild and open, it's filled with all kinds of animal life, including humans."

The audience laughs for some reason.

"The thing is, most people think animals are just here for our pleasure. They don't identify them as thinking, breathing beings. Those fishermen who murdered seals and sea lions, they just saw them as a problem. By the way, I really didn't catch them by myself. It was my Uncle Teddy, and my friends, both above and below the ocean's surface, who did most of the work. It sounds crazy, but those animals talked to me. I'm not sure how, and not in words, but impressions. It was a sea lion who found me when I was kidnapped and led the rescue team to my location. Other animals even risked their lives to save me."

During my speech, people shuffle chairs and talk for a few minutes, but soon the room goes silent, except for my voice. My ankles shake on the high heels and I lean on the podium for support.

"As unreal as it seems, today a buffalo, a moose, and a grizzly bear helped save us. Also, a young Blackfoot Indian boy came to my rescue and watched over me. Nature herself rose up to carry me."

I pause and the energy of the crowd settles around me. I'm sure they think I am totally demented.

Whatever.

"The point is," I continue, "Nature is this huge organism, and we're part of it. If we listen, we can understand what Nature is saying. Animals, trees, plants, rocks, all have a place on our planet Earth. If we destroy one element, or a whole species, we change our world forever. Many people think it doesn't matter, but I've read we actually lose dozens of species every day, most of them so small we don't notice. Think of the big species like tigers, or rhinos, what if we lost them? What if humanity were lost?"

I wipe my cheeks. *I must look like a complete* fool.

"Anyway," I say, "what happens to me is I feel the pain of an animal in danger. I don't know how, it just happens. And when I do, I can't help but act. Three months ago, I saw seals and sea lions in pain. I acted and they ended up saving my life. Today, a grizzly bear saved the President's life and mine. What if they didn't exist? What if, just because we didn't listen, we let them go extinct? We wouldn't be here, and maybe, neither would you. That's how nature works. One species contributes to the survival of another, and that species to the survival of another, and so on. When we save one, we save us all. Please, please do what you can to save our earth and all the creatures on it."

I close my eyes. Warm trickles slip down my cheeks.

"We are one. Thank you."

Total silence fills the room. The only sound I hear is the clicking of my heels as I, and the toy soldier, step back toward the table. The President begins to clap, then Uncle Teddy, and within seconds the room erupts. I wobble to my chair. People shout, "bravo," and, "well done." I put a napkin to my face and remember the animals who helped me. Their energy, their blood, pulses through my veins. I felt their spirit on the open plains, in the lakes, and in the forests of Glacier National Park and Blackfoot country. The musky smell of the grizzly filled me with each breath. The heavy, dusty odor of the buffalo surrounded me. The eagle's swoop lifted me. I was soothed by the soft rubber snout of the moose reaching out to rescue me.

For some time, I revel in the applause and sob into my napkin. I don't think I've ever been so connected to everyone like I am at that moment. I am one with everything.

Gradually the clapping disappears, and the President approaches the podium, his smile is for me. Eyes glistening with moisture, he speaks.

"Thank you, Samantha. That was beautiful. I had no idea you were a natural speaker," he laughs, "but why am I not surprised?" He pushes his handkerchief into his pocket.

"Today we all experienced, to one degree or another, a life changing moment. I had hoped to leave this meeting with commitments and plans for addressing our environmental challenges. Under the circumstances, I'll settle for an ongoing dialogue. This courageous young woman said it best. We will hear what nature is saying, if we listen. It cries out to us for help. Not just animals, but all of nature. Trees, plants, rocks, all have a place on our planet Earth. If we destroy a species, we change our world forever. And, what if they didn't exist?

The truth is, if they didn't exist, we wouldn't exist. Let us leave today with a renewed commitment to stop the extinction of species, and mitigate or eliminate the causes of Global Warming. Today we can begin the liberation of our planet, and all beings, from the disaster of climate change.

We are one."

Chapter Thirty-Three

An immediate shuffling of chairs and feet, and applause begins. Dignitaries press forward. It surprises me when they surround our little table, many hold out pens. At first I'm not sure what to do, but Uncle Teddy moves his hand in the air, like signing his name, and I get the idea. I spend the next twenty minutes writing on everything from booklets to napkins. My fingers begin to cramp and I pause. The President sits across from me, surrounded by Secret Service agents.

"You're stealing my thunder, you know that?"

"I'm sorry," I say, feeling myself blush.

He laughs. "Don't you worry. You are the best thing that could have happened."

I raise my eyebrows.

"You not only saved my life, you saved this conference. Every delegate pledged to continue this discussion with recommended actions."

The President stands. His back goes straight and I notice stiffness in his movements. He steps around the table. As I push up, he puts his arms around me.

"Something in the Native American tradition, I believe, says if someone saves your life they become family, or something like that. So, I think we'll have to arrange a trip to the White House so you can meet your extended family."

I push my cheek into his chest. I feel he isn't just talking. He means it. He relaxes and holds me at arm's length.

"Samantha, words can't thank you enough. What you did was beyond heroic. I'm leaving now, a country to run and all that, but I'll be in contact, and we will meet again."

He turns to Uncle Teddy. "And thank you, Ted. Your sound mind and quick action played an integral part in our survival. You have your country's gratitude."

The President looks from Uncle Teddy to me. "And Samantha, I won't forget about your father. You'll be hearing from me soon on that subject."

"And Runs with Fire?" I add.

He nods. "That is a more complicated situation, but I'll look into it."

A voice from behind me says, "Mr. President, we're ready."

I glance back and face the bulldog agent. A bandage on his cheek and his arm in a sling, he stands straight, his face as stern as ever. Strangely enough, I want to hug him. I don't.

"All right, Hank," the President says. "Let's get this show on the road. By the way," he says to me, "Agent Bere will take care of you from here. She'll make sure you arrive home safe and sound."

"Agent Bere? Like in Bear?" I ask as he wraps me in his arms again.

"Just a coincidence," he says. His warmth surrounds me. "We'll meet again."

His hand goes out and he pats backs and shakes hands as the bulldog guides him through the small crowd of dignitaries and larger group of armed guards toward the stairs.

I stare at his back for a moment, then I realize: *Oh my gosh, that's the President of the United States of American, and he said I'm his family.*

Chapter Thirty-Four

My skinny jeans slip over my legs without issue, but it's a major pain in the butt to get them buttoned. I pull on my Orca t-shirt and my tennis shoes. It takes only minutes to pack the rest of my stuff in my bag and backpack. Like before, I have to sit on the bag to fit my toiletries bag inside and zip it closed.

"I'm ready," I call.

"Give me about twenty, I'm going to take a shower," Uncle Teddy says.

Out on the deck, a cool breeze from Swift Current Lake brushes my hair. Fresh pine and fir fills my senses. From my perch, the lake reflects the silver of a new moon, and the large, triangular shape of Mt. Wilbur beyond.

My gaze wanders to the mountains. I imagined my friends in the forest. Bear foraging for berries, moose slobbering clumps of lake grass, deer nibbling leaves, fox hunting rabbit—each species contributing to the welfare of others through their own survival.

A rustle pulls my attention to a clump of trees. A rabbit avoiding a fox, I suppose. The smooth railing slips under my palm as I step down the stairs.

One last walk, just to say good-bye.

"Sammy," Uncle Teddy's voice follows me.

"I'll be right back," I say over my shoulder. "Be right back."

My feet take me along the lake shore, past the rustling grass and croaking frogs. A lazy dragonfly glides near me and I duck away from her buzzing wings. A fire red horizon brightens beyond Mt. Wilber to the west. Somewhere closer is Ptarmigan Tunnel where I met Runs with Fire, spirit or boy? I'll never know, but part of my larger family, I'm sure of that.

Beyond Ptarmigan Tunnel, the trail to Granite Park Chalet where I came face to face with my sister and savior, the bear, and Samuel. What do I do with Samuel, an idealist, or just a lying terrorist? I close my eyes and see his eyes. My heart aches. Is he my first love? Could I love someone who would destroy instead of build? Could I love someone who makes such bad choices? I don't know, but those chocolate brown eyes. I smile. Maybe, in some strange way, they're all my extended family, except Ark and Fatuma, of course.

A branch cracks behind me. I quiver, freeze, and listen. It wasn't bear or moose. This felt cold and steel hard. A glance back and I realize I'd walked farther than planned. The lights of the lodge twinkle through fir boughs a quarter mile back, to each side, darkness. My friends are not near, I know that. Another stick breaks and I spin around. His face appears like a ghost from a dream, followed by nervous laughter. He holds a pistol pointed at me. Out of the darkness steps Nakale.

OMG. Does this never end?

"I've been waiting for you," he says.

A sickening sweet smell of skunk weed rises up. The last edge of a pomegranate red sunset disappears and we're surrounded by darkness.

Trapped and caught in my own stupidity. Why did I take one more walk?

Nakale doesn't move. His face is blank, eyes searching. A million thoughts race through my brain. "I won't tell," I say.

"I know," he says.

My shoulders must shift, or my head. The gun thrusts toward me, his arm straight and shaking. "Don't move."

"They'll hear you, I say."

"You mocked me. You all laughed at me, and now…"

He chokes out what could be the cry of a beaten animal.

"I'm sorry," I say. "I didn't mean to hurt you."

My cell phone beeps and the blue light flashes inside my jeans pocket. My mind races for something to say.

"Want to hear a joke?"

Nakale cocks his head to one side like a bear cub looking in a mirror. His face softens and his eyes widen, either in curiosity or amazement at my idiocy.

"A joke?"

"Yeah. My brother sends me stupid jokes."

"Your brother is here?"

"No. He's back home, but he has this funny book and …"

As I speak, I slip my fingers inside the pocket of my way too tight jeans, and scissor the phone. I pull up. The blue light pulses off Nakale's eyes, wide, dancing from me to the phone.

"Can I read you one?"

Nakale's face remains stiff. He jerks as if reminded that he was the joke. "Stop," he yells, and steps forward.

I do as he says. "It's just a joke," and I show him the screen.

He stares at my cell phone with curiosity.

"Do you have family," I ask.

His eyes widen in surprise. "Family? No, my family was killed when I am a child."

"I'm so very sorry. My mother died a few months ago. Losing family is really hard, but I can't imagine what being alone is like."

"I'm not alone," Nakale says. His voice lifts. "I have friends too."

"I had to move," I say. "The one thing I miss most is not being with friends."

He smiles, like he agrees with me. "I miss friends too."

"Maybe I can be your friend."

He lowers the gun a few inches. His energy softens and his chin drops in contemplation.

"You? Friend?"

"Yeah, why not? I mean, you miss your friends and I miss mine. We could write to each other or something." Nakale struggles with the concept. I imagine his life as a kidnapped boy, forced to fight for diamond thieves. "How old are you Nakale?"

He stiffens. "Twenty … or twenty two."

I frown. "I'm only fifteen. Maybe you're too old to be my friend"

"No." He shuffles his feet, kicking pine cones. "Maybe I'm only seventeen, well sixteen."

It is my turn to smile. "Then we can be friends?"

His forehead creases, and his cheeks lift as he begins a smile. "Yes," he says hopefully, "I think we can be friends."

For a moment, it seems our conversation has broken the tension. Nakale relaxes, and is about to speak, when there is a call.

"Sammy," from the direction of the lodge, "Sammy."

"I'm here," I yell, my eyes locked on Nakale.

Startled, he jerks toward the voice and steps to me. He grabs the side of my neck. My hand rises; I swing in reflex. The edge of my phone case catches his jaw, leaving a red ribbon across his cheek. I struggle and pull away. Nakale falls forward, grabs my thigh and pulls me down on top of him. I push; his hands are all over me; he pulls and scratches. His gun, like a hammer, swings on me, and a sharp pain sears my neck.

"Nakale stop," I scream. "We can be friends."

I reach for his wrist and roll. Nakale is small, but powerful and quick. He rolls with me. His knees push in the dirt on either side of my waist, one hand on my chest and the other in the air. The butt of his gun aims at my head. I clasp my hands together to protect my face, and wait for the inevitable that will come with the impact of the pistol. Instead, Nakale freezes. His eyes fill with tears.

"We are friends," I repeat.

"Friends," he says. His chest heaves, and the assassin morphs from killer to child. Lights flash across the trail and sparkle in his eyes. The pistol drops and he rolls on his side, knees drawn to his chest, and arms wrapped over his head like an abandon infant.

"Sammy," I hear Uncle Teddy's voice.

Coughing, I twist and push to all fours. My arm reaches over Nakale and I grab the gun.

"I'm here," I say, and gently touch the center of Nakale's back. My hand pulses to the rhythm of his grief. "Thank you friend."

Three soldiers crash through the brush. Heavy boots fill the clearing. One drops to his knee, his rifle points at Nakale. Two others stop a few feet from me, rifles aimed at Nakale's head.

"Drop the gun ma'am," one says, without moving his eyes.

I lower the pistol to the ground as a steady thump-thud, thump-thud follows. Uncle Teddy appears, red-faced, limping on a crutch and hopping on one foot.

"Sammy, are you all right. What were you thinking?" he says, as he falls forward and, without meaning to, head-butts me. Before I react, his arms surround me, and pull my face into his shoulder. "I was so worried. I'm sorry. Are you okay? Oh gosh, oh my gosh ..."

He goes on for a while, apologizing, sobbing, and generally making no sense at all. Not only does my head throb, but I turn blue from lack of air. Struggling, I kick my way out of his headlock.

"I'm fine," I gasp. "You're killing me."

It would have been totally ironic if after kidnapping and attempted murder, my uncle smothered me.

The soldiers take control of Nakale. Without resistance, he lets them shackle his arms and legs. The only sound he makes is a low whimper. One soldier notices a blinking blue light in the brush. He reads the back of the phone. "Sammy Carlisle?"

"That's me," I say, and cradle the phone in my palm.

Single file, we follow the soldiers back to the hotel. Every so often, a light flashes through the trees and I wince at the sight of Nakale bent forward, arms wrenched behind his back. "He's only sixteen," I say to Uncle Teddy, but he is focused on hopping on one foot, and doesn't hear.

What earlier seemed like a ten-minute walk, takes almost forty-five minutes. Along the way I decide to explain why I left and what happened, but Uncle Teddy is too distracted and upset to listen.

Worked once, might work again.

About half way back I pull out my cell, blue light still blinking.

"Want to hear a joke," I say to Uncle Teddy.

That brings a faint smile. He pulls me closer and says, "Sure, why not. This whole day has been a joke."

I push the screen and Loren's words appear:

My eyebrows raise. "He's kind of psychic. Ready for this?"

"What do you call a bear with no teeth?"

Uncle Teddy shrugs, trying to look interested.

"A gummy bear."

As lame as it is, it brings a laugh from both of us.

Then I read the last line, "When are you coming home, stupid."

"There," I say. "The Dorkster returns."

Chapter Thirty-Five

The lodge sits like the mother ship, agents and military crawling all over it like ants. Light beams stretch from every window. Agent Bere meets us at the kitchen door and, with a slight limp, escorts us to the rattily old elevator. I hopscotch my way through the kitchen, careful not to touch blood stains on the floor, past several people in white lab coats brushing dust on pots and counters.

"Checking for fingerprints," Agent Bere says, as casual as if she does this every day. "We think we've captured everyone involved, but we'll continue investigating until we know for sure."

It hadn't occurred to me earlier, but as far as the government is concerned, this is an attack on our country, an act of terrorism.

"What will happen to the terrorists?" I ask.

"Depends," she says. "If this is considered terrorism, they could be sent to a detention Camp in Cuba, extradited to their own country, or tried here in the United States."

"What happened to the three who were in the hotel?" Uncle Teddy asks.

"We captured them as soon as they stepped off the elevator. They didn't put up a fight and will probably provide more information. They'll all be sent to Washington DC. Where they go after that is classified and above my pay grade."

I imagine Ark and Fatuma sitting in a small cell somewhere. Somewhere very hot, I hope. And what about Nakale? He's just a kid like me. Maybe he'll do better. Samuel? What will happen to Samuel? He'll be given medical care. After that? I expect he'll find a very small cell. I shiver at the thought.

On the rough wall leading to the elevator is a drop of blood. I reflexively touch my shoulder where only yesterday I cut myself. I chuckle. At the time, I had no idea what the next day would be like. We jerk up one floor. I start to ask Agent Bere if that is her real name, then decide it doesn't matter. I kind of like being protected by another bear. The logs in the fireplace sit dark and silent. Except for a few lab coats, the lobby is empty.

"We'll fly you out from here," Agent Bere says. "A chopper is standing by."

From the main entrance, we walk toward a small group of guards surrounding a helicopter. Over the hillside to the north circle two or three smaller helicopters, the glare of their spotlights on us, and the mountain to the north. I overhear one guard say, "News choppers. Like flies to honey."

Two agents lead Nakale to a separate helicopter across the parking lot. His head is pushed forward. As he passes he turns to me, about to say something. A Marine shoves him away immediately.

"He's only sixteen," I say, but no one listens.

Agent Bere hustles us away from the soldiers and Nakale, and almost throws me into the chopper. Uncle Teddy starts to crawl in behind me, but the pilot waves and extends his hand.

He turns to me, "Do you mind if I ride up front. I'd like to learn a little about this thing."

"No problem," I say. "I don't feel like talking."

Uncle Teddy swings into the copilot's seat as Agent Bere climbs in next to me and slides the cargo door closed. I notice our bags piled in back and I slip my ear buds out of the backpack. I push them in my ears as Uncle Teddy pulls on a pilot's headset. The pilot holds his thumb in the air, and we all responds with a thumbs-up. The cabin fills with a loud hum, the smell of oil, and the whup, whup of rotor blades. A moment later we lift. Light in front of the hotel disappears as the large double doors close, and sparkling window lights blink off.

The chopper hovers for a few moments, leans to the right, and within seconds the low chop of Swiftcurrent Lake slips below us. We speed over Granite Park Chalet, past Mt. Wilber, on our way to Loon Song Harbor. Like a dream, the most frickingly bad day of my life disappears below.

The cold plexiglass window presses against my forehead, vibrating to the spin of the blades. I imagine what it was like hundreds of years ago, before we invaded this land; animals of all kinds wandering free, hundreds of thousands of buffalo roaming the plains, glaciers covering almost all of what we now call Glacier National Park, and Native Americans, moving like the wind through it all. I pull my head back and the skin on my cheek pops as it comes unstuck from the glass, triggering a momentary memory.

"It doesn't matter, does it?" I say to Runs with Fire, somewhere below. "What matters is what we have today, and how we take care of it."

Agent Bere hands me a pillow and I lean against the wall. My last thought—*how could I have been so wrong about Samuel?*

Chapter Thirty-Six

A package, about the size of a small playhouse wrapped in red, white, and blue tape, arrives a week after we return. The sender's address reads: White House, 1600 Pennsylvania Ave NW, Washington, DC, 20006. The excitement I normally experience with surprises never appears. All I think is, *please don't be another invitation.* I can't take more adventures like the last one. Uncle Teddy, ribs wrapped in tight medical tape, and Loren, who is excited enough for both of us, manage to cut it open. Packages, folded in cellophane, fall out on the floor.

"It looks like your BFF is trying to replace some of your outfits," Uncle Teddy says as he tosses several bundles of brightly colored blouses, skirts, jeans and shorts on the couch. The plastic wrap crinkles when I tear open the end of the largest bag. A hoody appears with the emblem, President of the United States, on the back.

"Cool," Loren says.

"Yeah," I say without much interest. I hold up a pair of jeans with a round POTUS symbol on the back pockets. I scrunch my nose. "Not sure I'll wear these, but they're different." I set the jeans on the couch next to the other packages and my eyelids droop to close.

Loren pulls out a smaller box, an object the size of a violin, "What's this, what's this?" he says hopping up and down. "Open it."

I shake my head. "No thanks." Uncle Teddy cocks his head to one side. "It's okay," I say. "I'll watch."

Since we'd returned from the conference, I could care less about everything. Loren keeps pummeling me with jokes, and Liz encourages me to return to work at the dock store, but all I want is sleep, and my mind hasn't let me have much of that.

"You're going to like this," Uncle Teddy says when Loren rips the tissue back. "I'll be darned, a statue of your friend the bear, with a small plaque that says ..." Loren pushes forward and scrunches his eyes, "Pres-idential-Bear." He turns to me, beaming a broad smile.

While Loren hops around the statue, his voice disappears and everything in my vision pulls away. I have the sensation of falling backward into a deep, dark, hole. I flash moments of the battle at the farm on the Blackfoot Reservation, and a barrel points at my face. I freeze, and can't speak or move.

"Sammy? Are you okay? Sammy?" Uncle Teddy leans toward me. Loren hops in front of the bear, jousting and growling. My mind observes the movement and the question, but I can't hold on to them. Something pushes on my chest and my shoulders are heavy, as if someone sits on me.

"Sammy," Uncle Teddy says and touches my shoulder. I jerk and sit up.

"I think I'll go to my room," I say, and stand. Loren watches me from behind the bear statue. Uncle Teddy pulls back and searches my eyes. I turn, "I'm okay," and head to my only place of safety—my bed. "I'm fine," I say as I descend the stairs. "I just need some sleep."

I wake a hundred times during the night. Ark's fat nose pokes in my face, and the bullet from Fatuma's gun whizzes past me. Twice I hear myself scream and wake hoping Uncle Teddy hasn't heard me. My last dream is about Samuel, he has a gun and is shooting everyone, even me.

I wake with a start when our friend, Simone Dubois, bursts in. She told me about being an empath and I respect her as much as anyone I know, but I'm seriously pissed when she swishes into my room, no knock—nothing, and rips open the drapes. The room lights up like a wild fire. I squint to see her and pull the covers over my head.

"Now listen, Honey Child," she says with her Louisiana Cajun accent. "I'm sorry it took me a week to get here. She plants her ample butt on my bed and rubs my hand. Electricity crawls up my arm. "You've been through a whole passel of challenges lately. Most people would have sat right on the floor and cried their eyes out, but not you. You forged on. You're a trooper, that's what you are. Your Uncle Teddy, he's so cute, told me you stood facing a loaded gun, not once but three times, and had the presence of mind to run, duck, and even talk that poor boy out of shooting you. Oh my lord, you are a wonder."

Even with her beautiful voice and Cheshire Cat smile, I dread what is to come next.

"So tell me Sugar, how do you feel?"

There it is—the question.

When my Mom died, people didn't know what to say, so they asked questions, "How are you doing? Are you okay? What can we do?"

They meant well, and wanted to help, but all I could do was be silent and scream inside, "I'm doing horrible. I'm not okay, I've never been so miserable and there's nothing you can do—leave me alone."

Those thoughts take shape with Simone as well, but my scream never comes.

I stare at the comforter, silent, and wring my hands around the corner of a pillow.

"When my father died," Simone says. "I was in shock. He fell off our roof and landed right on his head. Looking back, it sounds funny, but it sure wasn't at the time."

A kind of laugh snorts through my nose.

"I was twelve, and he was the light and joy of my life."

I don't like where this is going, and squirm for relief.

"My sister and brothers seemed to get along fine," Simone continued, "but I went into a shell—someplace inside that was quiet and alone. I believed I needed to be alone. After weeks of me sitting in the bedroom, we only had one bedroom for four kids so alone was relative, my Auntie June sent for a priest. I was scared to death of that priest, let me tell you. He was tall and dark, with a head of hair that shocked the world. He wore a black suit and carried a huge Bible around like a baby. Until then, I only saw him on the pulpit preaching hellfire, and brimstone."

My gut contracts and I have the urge to pee. The words priest, and hellfire, catch my attention. Even though I don't want to, I listen to Simone more closely.

"One day, out of the blue, Auntie arrived with this preacher in tow," Simone continues.

"Sunshine, my nickname because of my high voice, Sunshine, she called as she waltzed in the door. This here is Mr. Solomon, a man of God. He's got some words for you.

When that preacher-man sat down in front of me, I was sure he would strike me dead on the spot. I shook like cat tails in a storm as he adjusted his suit jacket and set the Bible on the table with a thump. His gaze bore into me. I closed my eyes, and waited. I almost smelled the devil's burn.

'Miss Simone,' he began, 'I have come to talk with you about the death of your father.'

It shocked me to hear him mention my papa. Everyone in the house had avoided any reference to him since he died.

I opened my eyes and stared into the softest, kindest face I'd seen in a long time. He went on talking about what a tremendous loss I experienced, what loss does to a child, and what is expected in the future. He didn't sugar coat anything, just gave it to me straight. He knew that talking about what we experience is the only way to rid us of the demons that come with trauma. He was the only one honest enough to say the words death, pain, and anger. 'Loss, and the shock that comes with it, changes us forever,' he said. 'And that's okay.'"

I nod and feel the warm drip of tears on my cheek.

"Listen Sammy, we're worried about you. Not because you did anything wrong. You're amazing. It's because the trauma you experienced is eating at your insides."

The word trauma jerks me to attention. "What? I'm fine."

"I hear you think you're fine, but in the last three months you've experienced more traumatic events than many people experience in their entire lives." She paused. "Do you like me?"

I look into her eyes and realize what she means by, "the softest, kindest face." Simone's gaze wraps around me like a security blanket. "Yes, of course I like you."

"Do you trust me?"

My chin follows my nod.

"I'm not a psychologist," she says, "but I have some experience with human and animal emotion. And, you know I have some of that empathic sensitivity too. The experience

I had when my dad died, and what you're experiencing, is a type of Post Traumatic Stress Disorder."

My Dad flashes in my mind. "PTSD. Like my Dad?"

"Yes, similar I expect. Your Dad suffered trauma in war, and you experienced trauma in normal, well sort of normal, life. It's different, yet the same."

"But I don't drink or live on the streets," I protest. "What's the same about that?"

"Of course," Simone continues, her voice smooth and soft. "That is how your Dad is coping with what he doesn't understand. That is not how you cope. You cope the way I did, by going inside, digging deep in a burrow of silence."

My mind spins with her words. All my defenses fight to keep her words out, but I remember last night—how I sat on the couch and watched Loren and Uncle Teddy open gifts from the President of the United States. I re-experience their words fading and me falling backwards into that black hole. Simone leans forward, her arms wrap around me. I slump and lay in her lap as her fingers comb my hair. My head jerks when she speaks, as if I'd slept.

"Nothing can change the death of your Mom, the kidnapping two months ago, or the near-death experiences you had in the past week, but your relationship to them can change. All that matters now is how you see those experiences and how you feel about them."

"I'm fine," I say, as I shake my head and sit up, "I'm fine about what happened. I just want to forget it all."

"Yes you do, and that's what your Dad is trying to do. The problem is, Sugar, until your Dad, me, you, or anyone, fully deals with the memory of our specific trauma, we can't forget. You said you trust me. Are you okay if I make a suggestion?"

I gulp and nod, like my dry mouth is full of water.

"I'd like you to speak with a counselor, a trained therapist, who has a great deal of experience working with young adults who experience traumatic events, like you have. She's not a priest, I promise, just a very well trained and experienced professional. Everything you say will be confidential between you and the therapist. And, if you attend a few sessions, and don't like her, you can quit, no questions asked."

"I'm not crazy," I say, hoping that will end it.

"I know," she says, "but you need help to get through this. Trust me."

Every cell in my body wants to scream no, but something stops me. I hear the words, *trust yourself*, the dark hole recedes. Something relaxes.

My shoulders pull up to my ears and, as if I no longer have control of my body, my head nods in a silent yes. Simone wipes trickles on her cheeks. I smile as she strokes my hair, and lays my head on my pillow.

Therapist. What am I doing?

Chapter Thirty-Seven

Entering our kitchen is like walking into a sunroom. Light blasts through picture windows along two walls, and stainless steel appliances reflect like mirrors—pretty, but achingly bright. I slip on my sun glasses. Uncle Teddy stands at the counter, and Loren sits on a bar stool next to him.

"Morning Kiddo," Uncle Teddy says. "Feeling better?" Pancakes tower on a plate, and scrambled eggs and bacon sizzle in a pan nearby. "Hungry?"

My belly grumbles. I've been living on granola, bananas, and yoghurt for several days. "Yeah, I guess I am. Blueberries?"

"Yes, I have your fave. Liz brought them over this morning."

I shuffle toward the counter. The Presidential Bear stands on the red and white Formica table in the corner of the kitchen. Loren hops down and points to the bear's carved face. "He's smiling, see?"

In the light, I make out curved grooves forming facial features that are strangely familiar. "Look at his face," I say. I walk around to get a different perspective. "This is kind of crazy, but does he resemble the President?"

Uncle Teddy, who has been slathering butter on a stack of steaming cakes, smirks. "Yes, I noticed the same thing. I'm not sure if that was intentional, or coincidence. Just like the squat."

"The squat?"

"He's squatting getting ready to …"

"TMI," I say, raising my hand. "I can't think about that. Let's focus on breakfast."

The warm sweet smell of pancakes and syrup pulls me to the counter and I pick up a plate. "Did Simone talk with you about our conversation?" I ask.

"Yes, we talked before she met with you. I understand your first session is today."

His words catch me like a sneaker wave hitting my kayak. My anger builds and I considered my options: I'm not going, I'm too tired, or just yes.

"Today?" I finally say. I let the announcement soak it. "So you already made an appointment?"

"Yes, but we weren't trying to be tricky or anything. We just wanted to be ready. Simone suggested that there is no better time than right now to get started."

"You could have asked," I say. When he doesn't respond, I add, "I'm kind of nervous."

"Nervous about what," Loren says, pulling a pancake off the stack.

"Dorkster! What's the hurry?"

"It's all right," Uncle Teddy interrupts. "He's been overly patient waiting for you to wake up."

The clock reads ten-forty. "Sorry. I didn't realize. I must have fallen asleep again."

Loren bunny hops his way back to the breakfast nook, pancake flapping from his mouth, index finger pointing up in the number one sign. *What a total dork.*

"What time?" I ask.

"Your appointment's at noon. I planned on taking you."

I want to fight back, like I'm being pushed into something I totally don't want. Then I remember I said yes, and nod my head. "Great. I'd better get ready." I grab a pancake, roll a piece of bacon inside, and with all the enthusiasm of a cat entering water, I head for my bedroom.

We leave the coastal trees of Loon Song Harbor and drift through dairy farm land along the west leg of the island toward East Sound, the largest town on Orcas Island. I consider how I will sit and what to say, as we pass cows in pastures, and cars carrying kayaks or pulling fishing boats. We enter the village and turn off Main Street onto an alley with an ice cream store, coffee shop, and bakery. Her office is next door to the bakery. A small sign reads, Paloma Paislee, no title. The latch clicks and Uncle Teddy opens the door for me. A familiar aroma of Jasmine fills the room. It looks like my dentist's office except the chairs are nicer and there are no magazines on the table.

"Do you want me to wait here or at the coffee shop?" he asks.

I shrug. "I don't care. Here, would be okay."

He smiles, and an inside door squeaks open.

"Ms. Carlisle?

Therapy isn't anything like what I expect. Ms Paloma Paislee is about five feet tall and almost as wide. She fills the doorway when she walks through. I sit on a couch, and she sits in a huge overstuffed chair opposite me. I'm not sure how, but she sits cross legged. I expected a stern faced old hag, but she is young, like Liz, and laughs a lot. She reminds me of a sitting Buddha with her hands in her lap. She begins with a question. I expect her to ask me how I feel. Instead she asks me, "Why are you here?" After several minutes of me blaming everyone else, she rephrases it, "What is it *you* hope to get from this?"

The question takes me by surprise, because I hadn't thought about what I wanted.

"Sammy," she says, "this process is completely about you. I can be your guide and a resource for questions, but what you get from this will be all because of you."

Somehow, her saying that is like permission to focus on myself, and I begin to relax. We talk about what I want, for most of the session, and she says, "Before we end today, is there anything you want to ask me?"

My mind is blank until he crawls back in. I wet my lips and take a breath. "There's this boy," I say. "He's one of the terrorists, and he has the most beautiful brown eyes. When he touched my arm, I tingled. The problem is, he said he'd protect us, but he tried to kill the President, and..."

I go on for some time, way past the end of my session, until she asks, "And is there a question?"

I'm silent for a moment. "I'm an empath. How could I have been so wrong about Samuel? How could I have loved him?"

Ms. Paislee smiles. "Ah, love. Now we're getting into some serious business. The answer to that question may take a few sessions."

I nod. "Yes, but ..."

She raises her index finger, "But, we can talk about this in relation to your empathic skills. I'm not an expert, but from what you've said, your sensitivity is primarily with animals—bears, sea lions, whales. Right?"

I nod, cross my legs like her, and lean forward.

"Humans, I believe, are a much more complex animal," she continues. "We have likes and dislikes, and are driven much more by our emotion than most, if not all, other animals. Your empathic sensitivity works better with non-human animals because you are sensing their raw fear or joy. With Samuel, you sensed him through the filter of his emotions, and your own emotions. It is a much more complex process. And, if you felt love for him, that adds several more layers that no one truly understands."

I lean so far forward I have to catch myself from falling over. "Yes, I know. But I was so sure?"

She nods and her forehead wrinkles in thought. "I'm sure that is true. All I can say is you're not the first to be wrong. I've been sure a few times, and I still don't understand the process." When I sigh, she adds, "This probably doesn't answer your question, but be assured, we can continue this conversation until you find an answer."

She glances at her wall clock. "I have one more question, how do you see yourself?"

I'd never thought about it, but I surprised myself by saying, "I feel squashed, like a bear sat on me."

Instead of being all serious, she laughs. "Yes, I get that. Would you like to hear how I see you?" I nodded. "You're an egg, waiting to hatch into a beautiful bird. What bird are you?"

"A crow," I say, without hesitation. "I think crows are beautiful."

"And smart," she agreed. "Then crow it is. You are a gorgeous, smart crow, cozy inside your shell. When you are ready, you'll peck your way out into the world, but there is no hurry. This is your life, and you get to do it your way, in your own good time."

When she says she has an opening the same time next week, I answer before I can stop myself. "Sure, I blurt out, "I guess."

I'm a total idiot. Someday I'll have to learn to keep my big mouth shut.

I don't like the idea of therapy. I mean, I'm not sick or anything, but I do like having someone to talk to, and she has some pretty good ideas. Before I leave, she suggests each morning I imagine pecking on the shell of the egg. "Not to get out," she says. "Just to see what happens."

Chapter Thirty-Eight

It's been two weeks since Glacier. Other than some outrageous bruises on my legs, and a seriously sore butt, I'm feeling okay. I've seen Ms. Paislee three times and practiced the egg pecking thing. I haven't broken through yet, but at least I think I will—someday. Uncle Teddy is eager to drive me to my sessions, but there is a bus that runs from Loon Song Harbor straight to East Sound, so I think I'll take that next time—I need some space.

Mail keeps piling up. Uncle Teddy looks through it, and puts most of it in a huge bag in the basement. People who read about the Glacier Park incident write letters, most of them kind, the others Uncle Teddy throws away. The press keeps calling too. I haven't read the mail or spoken to anyone. Ms. Paislee says it's best to focus on taking care of myself right now—a weird idea.

Loren hasn't told me a joke in over a week. His last one was,

"What did one burp say to the other?

Let's be stinkers and go out the back door."

Uncle Teddy confiscated the joke book after that.

I still think about Samuel. I wonder how I could have been so wrong about him. I've come to trust my empathic sensitivity, but when it comes to him, like Ms. Paisley says, everything gets confused. Maybe Uncle Teddy is right about animals, yet I keep hearing Runs with Fire's words, "Do not doubt yourself. Trust your intuition. Trust yourself." *Who's right? Can they both be right?* I don't know.

The dock rocks in a smooth rhythm as I apply a coat of wax to the molded side of my dagger-like kayak. The sun beats down spreading warmth, a flock of ducks swim near inspecting my activity. Two crows caw from a tree just up the bank, and a boy waves to me from a small motorboat leaving the harbor. *Boys!* I look away.

Steps vibrate through the deck. "Hi Kiddo."

Sun shines around Uncle Teddy's blond hair and smiling face. "Just cleaning her up," I say as I stand. The dock stretches toward the bank with a row of sail boats, masts swaying and rigging clanking. I take a deep breath. "You know, we've never talked about the last time I went out."

"Yes, I figure we have plenty of time for that," he says.

"I'm sorry."

His brow creases in a question.

"I'm sorry for taking such big risks when you asked me not to. I should have listened."

"It's okay."

"No, it's important you understand. When I told you I'd only been out for an hour. I'd really gone out before sunrise. I used the animals as my excuse, but I know now that they can't save me from everything. It was stupid. Both going out alone and lying."

He nods, and remains silent.

"I also understand that I'm the only one responsible for my decisions. I mean, it was my fault and I won't do it again."

He rubs his chin. "I believe you. I know you mean this." He wraps his arm around my shoulder.

I lean into him. "Does that hurt?"

"No, I'm healing too," he says as he pulls me closer.

The safety of his arms gives me courage to continue. "There's something that's been bothering me," I say. "I mean about the attack at Glacier."

Uncle Teddy sits and pats on the dock. I sit cross legged facing him, and work to organize my thoughts. "I don't agree with anything they did," I begin, "but some of it makes sense. I feel really stupid for saying it, because nothing they did was okay. Still, I've done some research and the top one percent of the population own like forty or fifty percent of the wealth? It sounds horrible. I read yesterday that the bottom eighty percent of our nation own only seven percent of the wealth. I mean houses, cars, money, everything is in the hands of so few people, and a lot of people are starving, like Dad. It makes me feel kind of hopeless."

Uncle Teddy scratches the deck with a stick. He looks across the water toward San Juan Island and a large yacht crossing the strait. "It's like diamonds, isn't it?"

I look over my shoulder, "Diamonds?"

"Yes, the sun reflecting off the water. It always reminds me of diamonds on the water."

"Yeah, it's pretty."

"Kind of like the most beautiful place in the world, if I remember what you said at the conference."

I couldn't help but smile. "Yes."

"See that yacht," he pointed.

I nod.

"That yacht is sailing on diamonds and we get to watch. I'm sure they have a great view as well, and a heck of a lot more money, but right now we have the most beautiful view in the world, and it's all ours."

I squint one eye, "Okay, point taken. Some things are free. So what?"

He took a deep breath. "You are right about the disparity in wealth in our country and the world, and it's a huge problem. Many times I also feel helpless, but then I have to remind myself that we live in a country where it is still possible for a bumpkin like me to start a business, gain wealth, and do something good with it. Every time I think about the people who are hoarding their resources from everyone else, I remember the millions of young people, like you, who are spreading goodness around the globe. I remember the millions of ordinary people, like you and me, who raise great families, donate to charities or help others when they can. They truly believe that every positive action matters and will make a difference."

"Okay, I get that. But it's getting worse." I raise my hands. "it's not making a difference."

"Ark is a tyrant," Uncle Teddy says, "and his followers became terrorists because they believe violence is the only answer to the problems in our country and the world. A tyrant bullies people, threatens people, and if he doesn't get his way, he harms and kills people. Tyrants don't solve problems; they create worse problems and become dictators. Our economic system is capitalism. It's an imperfect system that requires a better system to regulate it. We are a republic and our political system is democratic. It's also not perfect, but we still have a say in our government and what it does. Banks and the rich may be too powerful, but I believe if we act on our values, and work for the changes we want to see— we can make them happen."

"Okay," I say. "What can I do?"

He laughs and slaps the dock. "The great thing about you is you are a natural."

I pushed my head forward in a silent, what?

"You just do what you believe is right. You see animals harmed and you act to stop it. You hear Ark talk like a demagogue and see him act as a terrorist and, before you can stop yourself, you open your mouth and argue with him."

"Yeah, a lot of good that did," I say, rolling my eyes.

"Yes, it did tremendous good. Who knows, you may have saved everyone in that building just by making a stand, voicing your truth, and taking action. We don't always know the results of our actions, but by following your heart, you live your truth, and that's the best you can do."

I rest my elbows on the dock, lean forward and support my chin, "It seems so big. I still don't think I understand."

Uncle Teddy scoots next to me and puts his arm around my waist, "I hear. To be honest, most of the time, I don't either. Just know, you are the most amazing young woman I know. You're not going to be perfect, but as long as you follow your heart, you can't go too far wrong."

"Even paddling out of the harbor alone?" I say.

"Boy, you've got me there," he says. "But yes, I trust you."

"Awesome. In that case, let me be honest about something."

His eyebrows worm up.

"I feel like going out in the kayaks—together."

He leans forward and twists to each side, exercising his ribs. "Okay, I think I can do that."

He takes a deep breath and waves his hand like he's swatting a bee. "Speaking of together, an email came today."

I look up suspiciously. He laughs. "As a matter of fact it's an invitation."

I flash an image of Ark. "Forget it. The last invitation you received ended up with us fighting terrorists."

"Yes, and we did a pretty good job of it. I'll let you read it later, then you can decide."

"Later? Okay, let me see it."

"It's not on my phone. Besides, it's need to know and all that."

I start to argue, but the patter of little feet draw my attention.

"Hey," clown-boy yells. "What are you doing? Can I go?"

There he is, dressed in purple shorts with yellow polka dots, green tennis shoes, a bright red shirt that reads, Glacier National Park, and his multicolored propeller hat. I reach out and spin the propeller. "Don't," he complains, but smiles.

I feel an impulse and kneel down. I reach out and clown-boy rushes into my arms. As my eyes water up, I realize what it would be like if something happened to me. I push my face into his neck and he squirms away. "You're sticky wet," he says.

I wipe my eyes and nod. "Yeah, you're right, I am. I'll be more careful," I say, "I promise."

Minutes later, geared up, we slide my sea kayak and a tandem kayak onto the water. I scoot my butt into the cockpit and attach my kayak skirt. Uncle Teddy struggles to maintain balance, as Loren wiggles, twists, and wobbles. I paddle out of the harbor and hear Loren, "quack, quack, quack," until we reach open water.

Like a porpoise, I sweep forward, skimming across the water quicker than, as Simone says, slip on slime. Several hundred yards out of Loon Song Harbor, a gray back rolls to my right and the whiskered face of a sea lion greets me. To my left, a spout, and the most amazing sight, the rise of the five-foot-long black dorsal fin of an Orca whale. Loren yells and points.

"Be careful," Uncle Teddy says.

My hand goes up, I wave, and pull long and hard. Fresh sea air and salt spray lift me. I whisper a silent greeting to my friends as my sleek red kayak skims ahead through billions of diamonds dancing on the water. A scream of joy erupts from my lungs—I can't help myself—I'm in my world now.

Letters From Sammy

Dear Reader,

Thank you for reading my latest adventure in Glacier National Park. Wow, I almost didn't make it back. I did though and I'm doing fine.

I thought you should know that I received a letter from Samuel, that man with the beautiful brown eyes. He sent it to Uncle Teddy's San Juan Express business address. Uncle Teddy didn't want me to read it, but he let me decide. I was really nervous opening the envelope. When I did, I realized I still liked him. Not him really, but his looks. I am totally shocked at how I could have been so wrong about him. I never imagined he was so messed up inside. He apologized and asked if he could continue writing. I'm thinking, *I don't think so, dude.* I've got enough on my plate already.

Uncle Teddy received an email invitation somewhere. I told him I'd had enough traveling, but to tell you the truth, I love it. I'm sure I'll find out soon enough if there is another trip in my future. There's no point in asking, he'll just say, "Need to know."

When I learn something, you'll be the first to know. Until then, as Runs with Fire said, "Do not doubt yourself, trust your intuition, and trust yourself."

Love

Sammy

Dear Dad,

I hope you are doing well. I am writing because you wouldn't believe who I met last week—the President of the United States. Yes, really! Uncle Teddy and I were invited to a G-20 conference on the environment in Glacier National Park. The exciting part is a group of protestors, really they were terrorists, crashed the party and … First, I'm totally okay and so is Uncle Teddy and the President. We're home and everything is fine. Anyway, this group of people rushed in with guns and a bomb. It sounds terrible, and it kind of was, but like I said, we're all just fine. You won't believe it, but I disarmed the bomb, I have no idea how, and the terrorists were captured. Uncle Teddy's plane, Angie, crashed and is being repaired by the Government. Uncle Teddy says she will be better than new.

When I got home I was feeling kind of depressed. Our friend, Simone, said it was a form of PTSD, something like what you have. I hope it's okay I say that. Anyway, Uncle Teddy arranged for me to see a counselor-therapist. Her name is Ms Paloma Paislee. I'm going to see her once a week. I like her and it helps to talk about what happened.

I guess that's about it for now. I hope this letter reaches you and you are okay. If you ever want to talk, Uncle Teddy is here, and so am I.

Love,

Your daughter, Sammy

The President of the United States of America

Dear Mr. President,

Thank you for inviting me and Uncle Teddy to your conference. It was very exciting. I'm sorry it didn't work out as planned, with the kidnapping and all, but I appreciate all you did to save us. Also, thank you for the Presidential Bear statue. It's hilarious. My little brother, Loren, and I love it, and I love the clothes you sent me.

I was amazed on how willing everyone at the conference was to work on global warming and climate change. It's an important issue my generation is very concerned about. I hope you will also remember what Runs with Fire said and have some time to work on our government's relationship with the Indian Nations. They are Americans too.

I know you're very busy, but you mentioned my Dad. He's having a tough time right now and anything you or our government can do to help him and other veterans suffering from PTSD is very much appreciated.

If you still want me to, I'd like to come to Washington DC and meet your daughters. I'm feeling pretty well, so I could to that almost any time.

Thank you again. See you soon I hope.

Sincerely,

Sammy Carlisle

Runs with Fire

Blackfoot Indian Reservation

Browning, Montana

Dear Runs with Fire,

I don't know if you will receive this letter. I am writing to thank you from the bottom of my heart for what you did to save my life, and the lives of Uncle Teddy and the President. What happened was really terrible, but you told me to trust in myself, and I did, and everything turned out okay.

If you want to, I'd really like to write to you, maybe text or chat or something. I don't know if you are on a social network or anything. If not, we can just write. That's kind of fun too.

I've included my email and Uncle Teddy's business address, on the envelope, so you can write to me if you like. I have so many questions. I'd love to be your online or pen friend.

Also, I'd really like it if you could visit us sometime. My very good friend, John Hania (Olie) Smith is an elder in Coastal Salish tribe of the Indian Nation. He also has spirit power. Maybe we can arrange that sometime. Thank you again and please stay in touch.

Sincerely,

Nitakein-Sammy

Dear Presidential Bear,

I know you will never see this, so this letter is more for me than you. Of all the creatures in the woods, you are my favorite. You are the most ferocious, protective, loving, and flatulently funny bear I've ever met, and I am eternally grateful for your protection. Thank you for saving our lives.

I promise, I will do everything I can to help protect the environment, and to protect endangered species, including grizzly bears, around the world.

I meant it when I said, "What if, just because we didn't listen, we let them go extinct? We wouldn't be here ... One species contributes to the survival of another, and that species to the survival of another, and so on. When we save one, we save us all."

I'll come back to Glacier National Park and visit, but until then I'll do what I can to save the environment in the San Juan Islands, right here at home.

Love,

Sammy

PS. Sometimes I feel like an endangered species too.

For more information on
Sammy and the San Juan Express,
to register for the Sammy newsletter,
and to tell us your favorite scenes
visit:

www.Empathteen.com

If you enjoyed Presidential Bear or the other Sammy stories
in the Empath series
please give us a review on Amazon.com and
Goodreads.com. Just search for
*Empath, Empathteen, Sammy and the San Juan Express, or
Presidential Bear*

Author

When not traveling, Nickolai Vasilieff can be found bent over his computer in a cabin, on the bank of the Necanicum River, in Northwest Oregon, USA.

Nick is a Navy veteran, private pilot, businessman and writer, who has traveled to over forty countries, including a one-year, around the world trip, living out of a backpack.

The Empath stories are partly inspired by those trips, the children he met around the world, and summer vacations in the San Juan Islands with his two children. The stories he made up during those summer vacations eventually evolved into the Empath series featuring *Sammy and the San Juan Express*.

"Young Adult novels are of particular interest to me, where the imagination of youth is combined with an insatiable appetite for knowledge and adventure, and where confidence is fragile yet boundless. Creating challenges through which characters grow in mind and spirit is a constant objective, along with spinning a good tale, of course."

Acknowledgements

My book required many eyes and much advice to complete. Each paragraph and chapter is the result of constant and often laborious reading by my wife and primary contributor, Janet. Without her feedback and constant encouragement, Sammy would not exist in print.

I also want to thank my primary editor, Vera Haddan, whose constant, perceptive advice and invaluable guidance assisted me through the wonderful process of the craft of writing. To those who read my manuscripts and offered feedback, I am grateful and humbled by your positive input.

All images used in this book are licensed or used by permission of the owner. I am grateful to Sally Lackaff for the use of her beautiful forest images as background for the book cover. More of Sally's work can be found at www.sallylackaff.com. The bear image on the cover is from Shutterstock; maps on the inside pages are from the National Park Service

(https://www.nps.gov/glac/planyourvisit/maps.htm)

and used under their disclaimer notice on their website: (https://www.nps.gov/npmap/disclaimer/).

The bear image used at the beginning of the Letters chapter was taken by me on a recent trip to Glacier National Park. Yes, you can get that close to bears in Glacier.

Resources

Learn more about Sammy's friends from these online wildlife resources.

National Park Service

Mailing Address:

PO Box 128
West Glacier, MT 59936
https://www.nps.gov/index.htm

Glacier National Park

https://www.nps.gov/glac/index.htm

As the Crown of the Continent, Glacier is the headwaters for streams that flow to the Pacific Ocean, the Gulf of Mexico, and to Hudson's Bay. What happens here effects waters in a huge section of North America.

US Fish and Wildlife Service. Forensics Laboratory. Ashland, Oregon. (Known as ACSI in Sammy and the San Juan Express)

http://www.fws.gov/lab/index.php

The U.S. Fish & Wildlife Service Forensics Laboratory is the only lab in the world dedicated to crimes against wildlife. Our crime laboratory is very much like a 'typical' police lab, except the victim is an animal. We examine, identify, and compare evidence using a wide range of scientific procedures and instruments, in the attempt to link suspect, victim, and crime scene with physical evidence.

Washington State University Bear Research Center

https://bearcenter.wsu.edu

The WSU Bear Research, Education, and Conservation Center is the only grizzly bear research center of its kind in the United States. Federal and state biologists responsible for understanding and managing wild grizzly bears occasionally wanted to use captive bears in their studies. Because few zoos have the resources or sufficient numbers of bears to obtain meaningful data, the WSU Bear Center was established.

Wildlife Research Institute, Ely Minnesota

http://www.bearstudy.org/website

Working with biologist Lynn Rogers, Ph.D., for over 40 years, the Wildlife Research Institute (WRI) is conducting the longest and most detailed black bear study and the largest educational outreach program ever done for black bears.

North American Bear Center

http://www.bear.org/website

The mission of the non-profit North American Bear Center is to advance the long-term survival of bears worldwide by replacing misconceptions with scientific facts about bears, their role in ecosystems, and their relations to humans.

World Wildlife Fund—Endangered Species

http://www.worldwildlife.org/about

The world's leading conservation organization, WWF works in 100 countries and is supported by more than one million members in the United States and close to five million globally. WWF's unique way of working combines global reach with a foundation in science, involves action at every level from local to global, and ensures the delivery of innovative solutions that meet the needs of both people and nature.

The Center for Whale Research. Friday Harbor, Washington

http://www.whaleresearch.com/#!orca-store/c1i6k

For four decades, the Center for Whale Research (CWR) has conducted an annual photo-identification study of the Southern Resident Killer Whale population that frequents the inland waters of Washington State and lower British Columbia. Since their initiation, these studies have provided unprecedented baseline information on population dynamics and demography, social structure, and individual life histories.

The Marine Mammal Center—Steller Sea Lions

http://www.marinemammalcenter.org

Steller Sea Lions

Steller or northern sea lions are sometimes confused with California sea lions, but are much larger and lighter in color. Males may grow to 11 feet (3.25 m) in length and weigh almost 2,500 pounds (1120 kg). Females are much smaller and may grow to nine feet (2.9 m) in length and weigh 1,000 pounds (350 kg). Steller sea lions are light tan to reddish brown in color. They have a blunt face and a boxy, bear-like head. Adult males do not have a visible sagittal crest (the bump on the top of their heads) as is seen in adult male California sea lions. Adult male Stellers have a bulky build and a very thick neck with longer fur that resembles a lion's mane, hence the name "sea lion.

Pacific Harbor Seal

Pacific harbor seals have spotted coats in a variety of shades from white or silver-gray to black or dark brown. They reach five to six feet (1.7-1.9 m) in length and weigh up to 300 pounds (140 kg). Males are slightly larger than females. They are true or crawling seals, having no external ear flaps. True seals have small flippers and must move on land by flopping along on their bellies. In San Francisco Bay, many harbor seals are fully or partially reddish in color. This may be caused by an accumulation of trace elements such as iron or selenium in the ocean or a change in the hair follicle.

The Seadoc Society—People and Science Healing the Sea

http://www.seadocsociety.org

The SeaDoc Society works to protect the health of marine wildlife and their ecosystems through science and education.

OSU Marine Mammal Institute

http://mmi.oregonstate.edu/whale-telemetry-group

Whale Telemetry Group (WTG)

The Marine Mammal Institute's Whale Telemetry Group (WTG) has pioneered the development of satellite-monitored radio tags to study the movements, critical habitats, and dive characteristics of free-ranging whales and dolphins around the world. Since the first deployment of a satellite tag on a humpback whale off Newfoundland, Canada, in 1986, the WTG has tagged a total of 462 whales from 11 different species. This work has led to the discovery of previously unknown migration routes and seasonal distribution (wintering and summering areas), as well as descriptions of diving behavior.

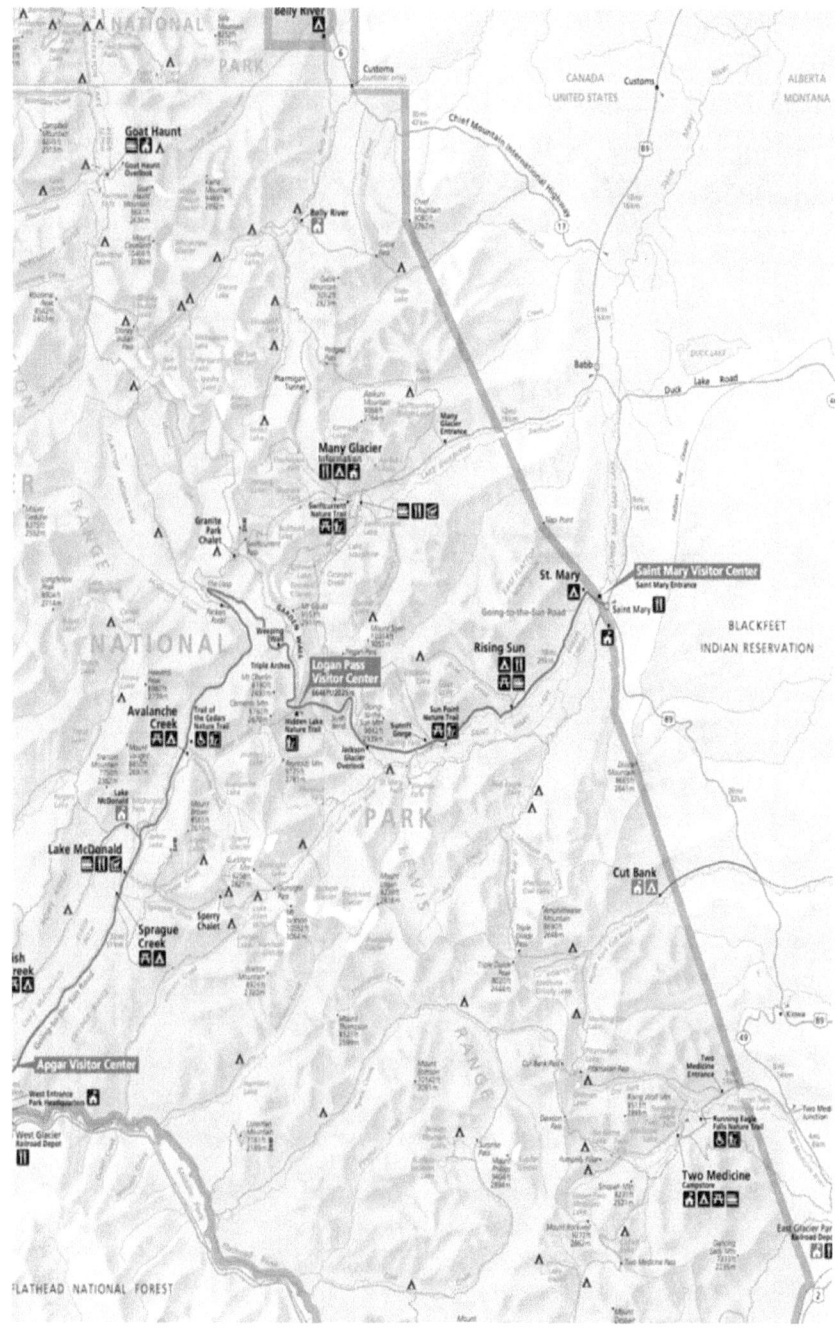

www.ingramcontent.com/pod-product-compliance
Lightning Source LLC
Chambersburg PA
CBHW050506260626
47157CB00004B/1212